Love Notes

Reginald Dunlop

Maxamillian Publishing

Maxamillian Publishing
A Division of the Maxamillian Group
P.O. Box 10034, Chicago, IL 60605

Maxamillian and the medallion are
trademarks of Maxamillian Publishing

All of the characters in this book are fictitious,
and any resemblance to actual persons, living
or dead is purely coincidental.

Cover Design by Yisrael Graphics and
Communciations

ISBN 0-9632749-0-2

Library of Congress Number 2003107844

Copyright 2003 by Reginald Dunlop
All rights reserved.

Printed in the United States of America
July 2003
First Addition

1 3 5 7 9 10 8 6 4 2

Lovers pave the way with letters.
   —OVID, The Art of Love

Chapter 1

Without any warning, it just happened. No black cat crossed our paths and no eerie red mist rose from over the lake. There should have been a dark voice coming from the sky or a sign telling us to turn back, but there was nothing.

The clock on the dashboard read 12:20 A.M. as I accelerated down the ramp and onto Lake Shore Drive. I had my window open, letting the warm June air from the lake rush past my face and dance around the car. As I looked over my left shoulder for traffic before entering the drive, I got a spectacular view of Chicago's skyline. The lights from the glistening skyscrapers shimmered and danced across the placid Lake Michigan waters.

Two car lengths ahead of me was my wife Marlena in Bessie, her Honda Accord. She loved Bessie and talked to her as if she were an old friend. I always thought it was cute when she would say things like, "I'll see if Bessie wants to take me to the store," as though she wouldn't go if Bessie elected to spend a leisurely day in the garage.

As I watched Marlena swaying and bobbing her head to the stereo through Bessie's rear window, I found myself smiling and shaking my head, especially when she lifted her right hand and waved it around like someone testifying in church. She was listening to Joe Sample. She only moves like that to Joe. I could almost hear the music as I thought about what everyone at our party said: Marlena and I had become so close that we no longer needed words to communicate.

We were on our way home from our thirty-fifth anniversary party. Marlena had suggested that we take separate cars so we would have room to carry home all of the flowers and presents that we usually received on these kinds of occasions. She was right, it was more practical to take both cars, but I argued against it, because I wanted us to ride together. It looked like everyone at the party had had a wonderful time, but for us, the night was still young. Every year we vowed to make our next anniversary night better than the last, and it was looking like we had done it again.

Marlena had prepped the bedroom before we left home. She had put the satin sheets on the bed and decorated the room with candles and roses from her garden. I had the champagne and strawberries chilling in the refrigerator, along with a surprise that I couldn't wait to break out. I was as anxious to get her home and into the bedroom as I had been on our wedding night. Our lovemaking, throughout the years, has evolved from the uncontainable fury and passion of young lovers to a slower, more ethereal savoring of each other that may start with a flicker of the eyes over coffee or a clever smile. Our anticipation of this evening had been building for days.

We had just passed the bridge over the Fifty-ninth Street marina when a wall of xenon lights appeared, searing my retinas like the flash from a ten-foot camera. Through the slits of my squinted eyes I could see Marlena veering to the right, away from the lights. I slammed on my brakes, which sent the car skidding to the left. From that second on, things happened in slow motion. The big sports-utility truck smashed into the front of her car, driving it off the road and into the girth of a waiting oak tree. I clenched my hands on the steering wheel, locking my arms while trying to jam the brake pedal through the floor. The high-pitched squeal of my tires turned into deep scrubbing sounds as the rubber ate into the asphalt. When the tires finally did take hold, the car jerked to a sudden stop, tossing me into the door and back upright in the seat. Thick white tire-smoke blew past the beams of my headlights and slowly thinned, bringing my nightmare into view.

For a moment I sat frozen in disbelief. Once the reality sunk in, I threw the gear selector into park and flung myself out of the car. I ran for a few steps before my legs turned to lead, slowing me to a stop. Marlena's car Bessie was crushed to half of its size, and the front end looked like some big creature had taken a bite out of it. Severed wires and hoses dangled hopelessly, while fluids dripped onto the ground. I crept closer.

The glare from my car's headlights on the shattered glass made it hard for me to see inside the car. As I got closer my legs nearly gave way when I saw Marlena's head pressed into the spider-webbed glass of her side window.

I grabbed the car door and yanked at the handle. Nothing happened. I pulled and pulled, then realized that it was locked. Panic raced through my body like a roller coaster screaming down the first drop. I ran around to the other side of her car to try the passenger door, but it was so bashed in that I knew that it wouldn't open. I tried it anyway and looked into the car through the shattered glass. I beat my fists on the door before kicking it several times. I took a step away from the car and twirled around, looking for someone or something that could help me, but there was nothing but cold darkness.

I ran back around to Marlena's door and pulled on it again, when I realized that I had a key to her car on my key ring, which was still in the ignition of my car. I ran back to my car in a haze. I snatched the keys out of my ignition and flew back to her car. I fumbled through the other keys on my ring until I got to her car key. I stuck it into the hole and tried to turn it. It didn't move. I jiggled the key up and down, twisted it left and right; still nothing. It was as if I had the wrong key. I pulled it out and checked the Honda logo. It was the right key. I took a deep breath, reinserted the key and twisted with both hands until I felt the key bending. I stopped and turned it back to the left and then firmly to the right.

At first I couldn't tell whether the lock was giving way or I was actually twisting the metal key. It was the lock; it slowly gave way. I lifted up on the door handle, but it must have been jammed. I looked down at the fluid dripping from the engine compartment and got a vision of the car exploding into a flaming inferno the way they do

Love Notes 7

in the movies. I fit both of my hands in the slot under the handle and lifted with all of my might.

I was certain that I was about to break the handle off when the door swung open and Marlena's body fell out and onto the ground. She came to rest against my legs, which turned to spaghetti.

I stood there, trying to stay balanced. I shut my eyes and took two deep breaths before opening them and looking down. Her hair was matted to her head like cotton candy with blood, dirt and broken glass woven into it. A small steam of blood had made it down her neck, the dark kind that comes from within—and her eyes were both open much too wide, like those of a mannequin or a ventriloquist's dummy.

My body began to shudder and I felt what seemed like a spike being driven through my chest. I tried to scream but my throat was locked. Blood rushed to my head. My lungs sporadically contracted for air, causing that spike in my chest to hurt worse. I grabbed at my chest, feeling for the spike, but it must have been under the surface. As the pressure built inside my head and my ears burned and my eyes bulged, my body let go.

I never felt the rock that my head landed on. In fact, I felt no pain at all. What I felt was a sense of calm and comfort that I had never experienced before. I could hear, feel, and taste the world around me: the trees, the insects, the birds and everything that was alive. I could smell everything in the air—moisture from the lake, sap from the trees, and the faint, musky smell of burning rubber. I was giddy and euphoric, like Peter Pan in flight, until I looked down.

Beneath me was Marlena's body in her formal gown, and my body lay next to her in the grass. We looked like two figures from a wax museum. As I wrestled to understand what was happening, I was startled by sinister-sounding voices below me. The voices were muffled, but I was able to make out that they belonged to at least two males, who sounded frantic and desperate. Just as

I was beginning to make out some of their words, they were drowned out by the sounds of a car engine cranking. The cranking started and stopped, started and stopped, until the driver let it turn continuously, draining the battery of its last bit of life. After the starter had turned its last turn, the sound of the voices returned, then the driver's door swung open and a dirty black teenager slithered out. After scrambling to gain his footing he quickly disappeared into the night. There was more commotion inside of the truck, before the sounds of another voice filled the area.

"Yo, Tre. My door's stuck. Hold up, man . . . wait for me!"

The first teen was long gone into the night before his frustrated accomplice was able to fumble his way out of the driver's door. I was trying to follow his black silhouette into the park with my eyes, when I heard the shrill of a siren. The ambulance came into view, screeching around the corner and accelerating toward the accident scene. The dancing array of red and white lights sent eerie shadows deep into the park. Once the oversized vehicle had chirped to a halt, a battalion of blue uniforms raced to the scene, one by one. Each paramedic was armed with a large black case. Three of them raced to Marlena's body and three to mine. The team around Marlena's body was methodical, but showed little excitement, while the ones who worked on my body were frantic. One of the men left Marlena's body and ran over to my body to help the team there. He was a tall, Italian-looking man; he began pounding on my chest with both hands, as though he wanted to break it. My chest caved and my arms and legs danced like rag dolls. Then there was some yelling between two of the men, before one of them opened a box and removed two metal plates with wires attached to them, which he placed on my chest.

When the first charge jerked my body off the ground, it shocked me into reality. I looked around me, and I didn't see any body parts. It was like being in a dream where you see everything except yourself.

My body had given up and they were trying to bring me back, but what about Marlena? Why weren't they trying the paddles on her? I wanted to get down there and tell those guys to forget about me and work on her—but where was I? It was as though I were watching this whole thing from the limb of a tree, when I felt myself being pulled away. I wanted to watch and see what was going to happen. I resisted with all that I had, but it was no use.

I began drifting upwards, like a scuba diver surfacing from the deep. In an instant there was no park, no cars, paramedics, or sirens. Those things were now miles behind me. I was ascending slowly through a rich, silky-blue essence, gaining speed as I came closer to the light.

The light was a warm and radiant translucent mass, which glowed from the center. It seemed to be moving within itself like different layers of clouds moving at different speeds. I wanted to race toward it as fast as I could, like a child returning home to his mother. My state of euphoria had become so frenzied that I was getting scared—but then I stopped moving.

I was stalled as though treading water when the first image came out of nowhere. It was about the size of a poster, and it floated through the air like an autumn leaf, before stopping in front of me. It was my mother's face; she looked into my eyes and smiled. My mother had passed away about twenty years ago. I looked at her picture almost every day, but this was the first time that I felt like I had *seen* her since she passed. I wanted to grab her and hold her next to my heart. I reached toward her image and it was as if the wind from my movements caused it to drift away. I looked around, puzzled, when the next image appeared.

It played like a video clip. This one was a scene of me at three years old, running around my grandfather's farm in his size-eleven shoes as he chased me, drunken with laughter as my grandmother looked on, smiling. Whenever we spent time with Grandma and Grandpa Brown, it seemed like all that my grandfather did was play with me, while my grandmother baked cookies and cakes. It was the best.

Next was an image of my father. It was a still shot of me and him sitting on the back steps of our home. It was on those steps that he would teach me about the world and about being a man. My heart grew warmer as I sat and stared at his face, when his image drifted away. For a while there was nothing else, as though the show had ended. I began looking around, the way you do when you see a shooting star and search the sky, trying to spot another. I was still scanning in all directions when a huge, three-dimensional image of Marlena's face appeared. In this image she was about twenty-three. As I looked into her glistening brown eyes, I was as mesmerized as I had been when I first met her. Her skin was as smooth as fresh honey, and her smile melted my heart once again. When her lips began to move, it was no longer some image, it was really her. There were no sounds, but I watched her tender lips form the words, "I've loved you from the day that I saw you." That's what we used to tell each other all the time. I told her that as we marched down the aisle and we've been saying it to each other ever since. As I gazed into her eyes and reached out to touch her, her face faded into another picture. As I watched picture after picture of her, I began to feel a presence near me. So much of what was happening was unusual, but this was like when someone sneaks up behind you and covers your eyes and it takes you a few moments to realize who it is. This time, it was Marlena.

What happened next was so amazing that my body shudders when I try to describe it. Marlena was not only with me, but she was around me, throughout me, fused into me as one. It was as if she had come up to hug me, but continued walking until she was right inside me. I was inside her and she in me. It was closer, tighter, and more intimate than making love, allowing us to express things to each other in ways that we hadn't been able to before.

I was able to let her feel what I felt the first time I touched her lips. She let me feel what she felt when she first saw me. She really did have butterflies in her stomach when she first saw me playing the piano: I could feel them. I was sharing with her how I felt when I proposed, when a new image appeared.

It was bigger, bolder, and more animated than the other images.

I felt her heart taking double beats. This image showed the two of us in our early twenties, walking in front of Buckingham Fountain at night. With Chicago's skyline as a backdrop and the amber lights illuminating the fountain's sixty-foot stream of water, I slipped the ring out of my right pocket and said one last prayer before dropping to my knees. *"God, please let her say yes."* She got to feel what I felt at that wonderful and scary moment in my life, and I got to feel her.

With our hearts and minds as one, we were able to feel some of the best things in our lives together. The first time we made love; the day we got pregnant; the birth of our children . . . it was incredible to feel what she was feeling at all of those special times. As we experienced each other's feelings during the first time we each saw our son Kenny, I noticed that we were drifting upwards, the way I had been earlier.

We must have been drifting upwards all along, because that warm luminescent light was so close that I could feel its warmth. The intensity of the love around me, from Marlena and from the light, was intoxicating. Because I had also been feeling the joy in Marlena's heart, I was shaken when I felt an influx of pain and darkness invading her. Everything began to darken, and we stopped moving up toward the light. I felt the difficulty and uneasiness in her body as she prepared to tell me what would shock both of our souls.

"Honey," she said, as her soul quivered, "I feel so happy and blessed that God gave us this special time that we've had, but you can't continue on with me. It's not your time to go, but it is mine."

The world froze. The warmth, the closeness, everything was in disarray. I wanted to stop her, cut her off in mid-sentence and tell her that my place was with her, in heaven, on earth, or anywhere in the universe, but my voice had no sound.

"There are things on earth that you must do. Our children will need you now more than ever. They are grown, but they need your wisdom. They need you to teach them what we know about this life. Hosea, I will be here for you when it is your time and we will be together as one, forever. But now, Baby, I have to continue on."

I still couldn't speak. I stood silently as she floated away like a lost helium balloon in the park.

* * *

"We've got a pulse!"

"He's breathing," another voice cried out.

I sensed the bodies around me. They were noisy with chatter and frantic conversation. I felt my body, but was unable to move.

Suddenly my right eyelid was pulled back and a beam of pure white light probed the back of my eye, then it stopped. I was moving, being rocked from side to side. I eased my eyelids open myself this time to see what was going on. I was in a very small area surrounded by people in uniforms.

"Mr. Brown?" A voice came from one of the faces.

I tried to open my eyes further, but the brightness of the light prevented me from opening enough to see who was talking.

"Mr. Brown? Can you see me?" he asked frantically.

I tried to focus. He was a clean-shaven Indian man who was holding what looked like my wallet. There was pressure on my chest; I felt like my body was in cement.

"Can you hear me?"

My eyelids closed, but I forced them open again.

"How many fingers am I holding up?" a woman's voice asked.

I tried to say two, but nothing happened.

"Nod if you understand what I'm saying," a third voice said.

"Do you know your name?"

I think I moved something on my body.

"Is it Hosea Brown?"

I tried, and I think that I was nodding, but it was hard. I began to fade.

"I don't see anything on this emergency card here in his wallet. Mr. Brown, are you allergic to any medication?" a different voice asked.

"Stay with us Mr. Brown," the lady's voice pleaded.

I tried to get my eyes to open, but they wouldn't.

"He's going out," a voice said.

"Mr. Brown, stay with us," another pleaded, but the voice trailed off like the last notes of symphony and everything went black.

Chapter 2

Shards of ammonia pierced my brain, shocking my eyes wide open. I was being pulled out of the ambulance and wheeled across a ramp. My head felt like it was splitting with every bump. I began to fight for reality. Nobody said anything to me as they pushed me along. I was being wheeled around a hospital, but why?

Being in the hospital was surreal. People talked to me and asked me questions, but I was in a haze. Every now and again, a doctor or nurse would open my eyes and shine a flashlight in them. I was numb and unable to talk or move. The few things on my body that I could feel were seared with pain. I felt my mouth moving or mumbling something.

"Did you say something?" one of the hospital workers asked.

"What's happening?" was all that I could get out.

"You were . . . well, it looks like you had what we call sudden cardiac arrest."

Flashbacks of the accident scene shot through my mind, before I faded again.

"Marlena!" I shouted, trying to free myself.

"Oh, my God, help," I cried, feeling the pain in my chest.

"Calm down!" the nurse pleaded.

"Where's my wife?" I asked.

She and the man next to her looked at each other, and then they looked at me with identical blank stares.

"Are you in pain?" the nurse asked.

Before I could answer, I felt a needle piercing my arm. The hot narcotic raced through my veins, my head became light, my body began to melt, and everything went black once again.

There was a dense fog in my head that I tried to shake as I became conscious again. I took a minute to take inventory of myself. My head throbbed, my chest ached, and my mouth was as dry as dust. I looked around the sterile room, trying to get a handle on what had happened. I shut my eyes and tried to focus my mind to get some sort of recollection. There was an accident in the park by the lake. Marlena's Honda . . .

Suddenly I had a horrible vision of her car smashed like a can, the windows shattered, her body slumped over the wheel. My heart began to thunder. Maybe it was a bad dream, I tried to tell myself, but something deep in my gut knew better. The adrenaline accelerated through my veins and questions flooded my mind. Was she all right? Where was she now? What about Kenny and Kara? Where were they? What had happened to me? Why was I banged up? I needed answers now.

One thing that I did know was that I was in a hospital and there had to be some way to call the nurses or doctors for help. I looked on the wall and saw some kind of port or speaker, and then I noticed the thick white cord clipped on to the bed. I pulled the cord until I got the remote control and pressed the button marked "nurse."

"Yes," a voice answered over an intercom.

"Can you send someone?" I asked. "I have a few questions."

"Right away," the nurse said.

I looked at the window, trying to get a sense of what time of day it was. The shades were drawn, but there was no light slipping through the cracks. It could have been dusk or dawn or a gloomy day.

"Good morning," a perky blond nurse said as she entered the room. This was not a good morning for me, I thought, but I still didn't know how bad it was.

"How are you feeling?" she asked me in a voice usually reserved for kids.

"Okay," I answered. "Where am I?"

"You're in the University of Chicago Hospital," she said proudly. She was now standing right next to my bed, looking me up and down.

"How does your head feel?" she asked.

"It hurts."

"You've had a mild concussion, and it's going to hurt for a while, but we'll try to make you as comfortable as we can. If the pain gets too bad, I'll call the doctor and see if he can give you something for it."

"Where's my wife?" I asked.

"I don't know, Mr. Brown. I can check the visitor's sign-in sheet to see if she's in the waiting area," she said with a contrived smile.

I could tell that the way I looked into her eyes made her uncomfortable.

"Okay. Check to see if my children are on that list. Their names are Kenny and Kara Brown."

She smiled when she heard the kids' names, as if she were pleased to know that I had children.

"What time is it?" I asked, still studying her expressions.

"It's 6:10 A.M. I'll get the doctor," she said, heading for the door.

The accident flashed into my mind once again.

"Nurse? Check to see if my wife is checked in here."

She stopped at the door and turned to answer me.

"I'll get the doctor," she said, trying to get away.

"Is Marlena Brown a patient here? Nurse?"

I heard her soft-bottomed shoes squeaking across the floor as she scurried away.

I sat up in the bed, looking around the bland room for something to distract me while I waited. Our anniversary party was now clear in my mind. There had been so many speeches and toasts and stories that touched me in so many ways. I don't think my kids or my wife had ever seen me cry. I'm the strong rock, Hosea Brown. My son, Kenny, is a tough-guy lawyer, but when he stood up at our party and delivered the first toast about the love in our home, I could see a few tears glistening in his eyes.

"Everybody, I'd like to propose a toast. I'm thirty-five; I'm a single black man with a good job. 'Why aren't you married?' I always hear. Why? Because my parents, Marlena and Hosea Brown, have set such a standard for love, marriage and family that it makes it hard for an average type like me to live up to.

Finding a woman with the qualities of my mother is like trying to find a needle in a whole field of hay, and for me, I have to keep working to have the intelligence, strength, and warmth to get a woman like my mother. Mom, Dad, you are truly the best. I want to be like you some day, and I thank you for making me and giving me such a wonderful sister. I love you all to death. Happy anniversary!"

Kara's tribute to us was sweet and elegant. There were also a lot of funny things from our friends, but when Marlena looked into my eyes and told me that God had taken one of my ribs to make her, like he made Eve from Adam, I shut my eyes to fight back a tear and ask again what I had done to deserve all of this.

The wait was driving me crazy. I could no longer distract myself. I needed to know now. This second! What was my life going to be like? Just as I was finishing saying a little prayer, asking for Marlena to be okay, I heard heavy footsteps. These were solid feet that owned the hallways. Then they entered my room, two men: one a doctor and the other . . . a priest. They walked deliberately, shoulder to shoulder like men on a mission. I could hear that they had been talking in the hallway, but they were silent when they entered my room. They marched right next to my bed and stopped.

"Mr. Brown."

I sat up fully erect in the bed.

"Yes."

"My name is Doctor Tenowsky and this is Father Lejess, the hospital chaplain. Mr. Brown, the soreness in your head will go away. You sustained a mild concussion from a rock that you must have hit your head on, after going into cardiac arrest from what we believe was shock. How are you?" He asked in a business-like fashion.

"I'm fine. I . . . my head hurts, but that's getting better. Doctor, I need to know about my wife."

"You were technically not with us for about five minutes and that often leads to disorientation," he said.

"Yeah. I have a bit of disorientation; things are becoming clearer, but my wife. I want to know about my wife."

My headache disappeared and my body became numb as I awaited his answer.

The doctor didn't hesitate. "I am the doctor who admitted your wife last night," he said. "There was nothing that I could do. She had lost a lot of—"

I didn't hear anything after *"there was nothing that I could do."* I collapsed as if someone had ripped the bones from my body and tossed me into a lake. I was sinking rapidly, drifting further away from the sounds and realities of where I was. This was what I had been aching to hear. Deep down inside, I had already known it. There was a part of me that knew that she was gone, but I needed it to be official. I needed for someone to remove the last sliver of hope from inside me, but deep down inside, I knew.

I knew when I saw her body in the car, crumpled against the wheel. I knew when her body fell onto mine. I knew when she left me and continued up to the light. I knew, but my mind wouldn't let me accept it while there was still a chance that I could have been wrong. There was a chance that things weren't as bad as they looked. She could have been in the next room, watching an old episode of *The Cosbys,* and all of this could have been a bad dream and we would all be going home in a few hours. But now things were as clear as crystal. The life that I had enjoyed for the last thirty-five years had ended less than twelve hours ago.

The father prayed with me long and hard. There were times that his words made me feel better and there were times that they made me feel bad.

Lord, if you are so kind and loving, why did you let this happen to my family?

I felt a little distant when Father LeJess began to pray with me. That distance probably came from my growing up in a sanctified church where we screamed, stomped, and got the Holy Ghost and believe that Catholics and others who sat reverently in church were somehow less holy. Father LeJess, however, was everything that I needed. He prayed and spoke to me in a way that gave me the strength to at least sit upright and gain some composure. Just as I had gained enough strength to sit up in bed, a new pain erupted in my heart. My kids—Kenny and Kara!

I lost it again and collapsed back onto the bed in a ball of tears. I call them kids, but they are adults. Kenny is 35 and Kara is 34. Even being adults I don't think will help them cope with the loss of their mother any better.

After my downpour of emotions had subsided, I pulled myself upright enough to talk. I looked at the father.

"I have two children," I said.

"How old are they?"

"They're thirty-four and thirty-five. They were very close to their mother. Especially Kenny, he . . . "

"Do you have pictures of them?" the father asked, cutting me off.

"Ahh . . . yeah. Yeah, in my wallet, wherever that is."

The priest began searching around the room, opening a few drawers as he looked for my wallet. Even though I knew what he was doing, trying to divert my attention to my kids, it was working. He pulled the wallet out of the nightstand drawer and handed it to me. I opened it up and the first thing that I saw was Marlena's picture. I felt my face become flush, and I froze.

"You got it?" he asked.

"Yeah." I took a deep breath and then flipped past Marlena's picture to ones of Kenny and Kara.

"Let me see that," he said. I held the wallet open while he took a corner of it and looked on.

"Good-looking kids. Kenny, is that it?"

"Yeah."

"He looks a little like Sydney Poitier."

"Yeah, he does. Marlena has . . . uhh . . . had a friend who used to say that every time she saw him."

"And your daughter is just gorgeous."

"Yeah, that's my baby. Marlena and I used to say that she took the best of both of us. Her skin color is right in between both of ours. Those eyes are Marlena's."

"She's got your nose," he said.

"Yeah, and all of that hair."

We both paused, looking at their pictures.

"I don't know how I'm going to tell them."

"I can help you," he said. "I can tell them for you, or I can be here with you when you tell them."

"Thank you," I said, holding his arm. "I think that your presence would be too much. You know. I don't want them to walk in and see a priest. You know what I mean?"

He nodded his head.

"Somehow I'm going to have to do this myself."

"Hosea, from my experience, I have found that there is no good way and there is no easy way. The best way is to just say it."

"Thank you, Father." I tightened my grip on his arm and then let it go. He looked at me and patted the top of my arm gently.

Love Notes 33

"I'll be here if you need me," he said before walking out.

I grew up being told that God won't give you more than you can bear. Back then nobody dared to challenge those old sayings. The loss of Marlena was more than I could bear, and I knew it was more than Kenny and Kara could bear, so where on earth was the clown who made up that one?

I ran at least ten different scenarios in my head of how to tell my kids, and what I would say, but none of them felt right. I practiced saying it in my head and out loud. Finally, I put it in God's hands and ask him to give me the right words to say and the strength to say them. I figured that was the least that he could do.

I picked up the phone at 7:45 A.M. and called Kenny. It rang three times before I heard his message. *"Hello. This is Kenny. Leave a message and I'll get back with ya. . . .* beeeeeep." I hadn't even considered the possibility that Kenny may have not been home or answering his phone. I still had the phone to my ear and felt like I was on the spot. The beep had sounded; it was time to say something. I started to say something, but I wasn't ready. I hung the phone up and stared into space.

At thirty-five, Kenny was still a man about town, playing the field. He seemed to be enjoying his life as a single black man, swaggering around Chicago. Maybe he was really looking for Ms. Right, like he said at the party, but it was hard to tell from looking at him.

When Marlena and I left our anniversary party, I had noticed that one of Kara's friends had taken a liking to Kenny and Kenny to her. They were at the bar, drinking colored martinis, laughing and exchanging flirtatious looks. After replaying in my mind that scene of the two of them at the bar, I was convinced that they were together somewhere. Either he had gotten a room there at the Hyatt, or he was at home not answering his phone, but I was sure that he was with her.

My plan was to get hold of Kenny and tell him to go get his sister and then have them both come to the hospital so I could tell them at the same time. I looked at the clock and thought about my next move. My eyes began to well up with tears. I tilted my head back and shut my eyelids firmly in an attempt to push the big teardrops back into my head.

I dialed Kenny one more time, and again I got the machine. I paused with the phone in my hand and then dialed Kara.

"Hello. Leave a message and I'll call you back. Ciao."

As soon as I heard her voice on the machine, I began to see her as she had been when she was my little girl, with those big brown eyes that glistened like stars. I knew that she wouldn't be home when I called her. On a Saturday morning, she was either running, biking along the lake, or in her office getting a jump on the week.

I caught myself and tried not to wonder what Marlena would do in this situation. She always knew the right thing to do when it came to the family. I picked up the phone and dialed

Kenny's number again. As the phone rang, I remembered that he had caller ID and might not be familiar with the hospital's number. Once his voice mail greeting ended, I left him a message. "Kenny, this is Dad. I need for you to call me right away. Your mom and I were in an accident last night. Everything is gonna be all right. Call me back at 299-9233. That number is the direct line to my room." I set the phone down and shook my head. "Everything's gonna be alright. Really now," I said, mocking myself.

Will it ever? How will everything be all right? *Your mother died last night, but everything's gonna be all right. I lost the most important thing to me on earth, but everything's gonna be all right.*

Not five minutes went by before I was startled by the phone. I looked at it and knew that it was Kenny. As I brought the phone to my ear, I tried to change my demeanor before speaking.

"Hello?" I answered, trying to sound okay.

"Dad?"

Love Notes 37

"Yeah, it's me."

"What's going on? You and Mom were in an accident? What happened?"

What happened? I wish I knew.

"I want you to get hold of Kara and come down to the hospital. I'm at the University of Chicago Hospital in room 513."

"What happened?"

I tried not to pause too long.

"I'd rather you guys came down here so we can all talk about it in person. I tried to call Kara at home, but she didn't answer. I don't know her cell number off the top of my head."

"How's Mom? Is she alright?"

"We'll talk about everything that happened when you get down here. Okay?"

"All right. I'll find Kara and we'll be right there."

I figured that the fastest Kenny could track down Kara, pick her up and be over here in Hyde Park would be forty-five minutes. That would give me time to figure out how I would tell them. As I played a few more scenarios in my head of what I would tell them, strange memories of the accident seeped into my mind. I felt as if somehow I had seen everything from overhead: the car, the SUV, and what looked like both of our bodies. I tried to dismiss those images and stay focused. I imagined Kenny and Kara walking into the room—Kenny marching right to my bed, ready to ask a battery of questions, and Kara with her scared little girl face. I took a big breath and imagined them at my bedside, silently studying every corner of my face.

"Hey, guys . . . I am glad . . . " No hey, guys. No. "Kenny, Kara, can you have a seat? I've got something that I want to tell you." Like I've got a big secret. Okay. No introduction; just start saying it.

"On the way home last night a truck pulled out in front of your mother and . . ." My mouth began to quiver. " . . . and it . . . ran . . . in . . . it ran in . . . to . . ."

The tears turned my vision into a kaleidoscope of blurry colors. My head dropped back to the pillow and I cried from the depths of my soul.

As quickly as they had started, the tears stopped. I looked at the clock and figured that I had another twenty minutes before the kids came. I decided the best scenario was to make sure that they pulled up chairs so they were seated when I told them.

I turned on the TV and looked at whatever was on. I might as well have continued to stare at the blank screen. I switched through a few channels before turning it back off.

"How could this be happening?" I asked, hoping that a voice from above would insert an explanation. I sat there quietly, but there was no answer. "What did we do to deserve this?" I asked. "What?"

I looked up in the air for an answer, but I didn't hear a thing.

* * *

I was sitting upright in the adjustable hospital bed as though I were in a giant chaise lounge when Kenny and Kara walked in. Heat began to rush through my body and I started to tremble. They walked toward me slowly and cautiously with their eyes fixed on mine. My lips started quivering so much that I wasn't sure that whatever I said would be decipherable. Kara's mouth dropped.

When they got next to my bed, I lunged at them and clutched them with all that I had.

"She's gone," I blurted out and I squeezed them even harder.

"Noooo!" Kara shrieked. I was twisted to my right side in an awkward way, but I held on to her. Kenny tried to break away, but I kept my grip on him. He was still for a moment and then he broke away. I took Kara in my right arm and sat as upright as I could. Kenny paced the room.

"Oh, God, no!" he repeated, over and over again. I watched helplessly as he paced around. Like a spinning top that was running out of steam, his pacing circles slowed down until he let himself fall down onto the bed and into my left arm. I was now on my back and I had Kara halfway on the bed in my right arm and Kenny on my left. Their warm tears quickly soaked through my bed gown as I felt their hearts breaking in my arms. I felt Kara slipping from the bed, and I think Kenny did as well; I pulled her up so her body was lying across mine.

I didn't know how strong I would be in this situation, but I had hoped that I would be stronger than this. I could feel Kara and then Kenny, in the midst of their tears, stop to look up at my face. I didn't know what I needed to look like or what I needed to say; I just sat there looking pitiful.

No one said a word or moved for fifteen minutes or more. It was silent except for an occasional sniffle. Kenny got up and went to the bathroom and returned momentarily with a box of Kleenex and put it on the bed.

His voice softly parted the silence.

"What happened?" he asked.

As I got ready to answer, Kara lifted her head up from my chest and looked into my face. The broken look on her face made me rethink what I was going to say. I could see that they couldn't take much more. I softened the story and told them a condensed version, which ended with me telling them that their mother was in heaven.

"What happened to you?" she questioned with the tenderness of a six-year-old.

"Well, a couple of things. The biggest, they tell me, is that when I opened the door of your mother's car, the shock stopped my heart for a few minutes and I must have fallen and hit my head on a rock. I'll be all right," I told her. "Yeah, I'll be all right. I have a little burning on my chest. I guess that they used those paddle things." I made a motion with my hands like I was using the paddles and Kara winced.

"What happened to the person who hit her?" Kenny asked calmly but with a tinge of brewing anger.

"They ran away," I said with a distant stare, as I tried to figure out how I knew what had happened. I could see it as if it were happening that moment: two skinny kids in their early twenties, plopping out of the driver's door one-by-one and running for their lives.

"Dad?" Kara's voice slipped in.

I snapped out of my daze and looked down to see Kenny and Kara looking into my eyes. I looked at Kenny, who started to say something but refrained. Kara suddenly erupted into tears. Kenny moved over to console her, while I sat there wondering what to do.

I tried to think of what Marlena would do. She always knew how to console us. I was on my own, and I would have to try to use her wisdom from what I thought that she would do from now on. I reached into the nightstand and grabbed the Gideon Bible. I sat farther upright in the bed. Kenny looked at me then and then back down at the Bible. I began reading as fast as I could.

Chapter 3

10 DAYS LATER

The wake, the funeral, relatives, and guests left me tired and numb. I had been staying at Kenny's apartment since coming home from the hospital. He and Kara wouldn't let me go home out of fear that I might have a big reaction. I was concerned as well about how I would react to the house and everything inside of it, but it was time for me to go home. I was apprehensive and nervous, but anxious for the experience, too. What would I feel when we drove up to the house? Would I be able to function after seeing the garden that she loved? I wanted to know where I really stood. If I was going to break down, I wanted to get it over with now.

Kenny insisted that I stay at his apartment for at least another night. I argued that it was time for me to face the music. We came to a compromise. The kids agreed that I could go home only if one of them spent the night with me. Kara said that she wasn't able to be in the house yet, so Kenny got the babysitting job. At first I thought that it was cute that they were looking after me the way that they were, but then I realized that I might not have been thinking as clearly as I should.

When Kenny pulled the car into the driveway, I became jittery. On the left was the crescent flower garden next to the house where Marlena had spent hours on her hands and knees, caring for her assortment of roses. So many of them were in bloom. They were amazingly beautiful, like everything else that she touched. In the brief moment that it took for us to drive past those flowers, she would have spotted a weed that had popped up or a leaf that needed pruning and taken care of it as soon as she got out of the car, no matter the time of day or night. She would leave the trunk open if we had groceries and go into the garage and grab her little pruning shears to clip that one leaf that was out of place on one of her babies.

I shut my eyes and took a couple of deep breaths. "I can do this," I said to myself.

When Kenny came to a stop in front of the garage and shut off the engine, I felt perhaps I wasn't ready to go inside.

"Dad, are you alright?" he asked. I felt as though I needed a few minutes, but Kenny still had his hand on the ignition key, so I knew that if I paused, he would have started the car and been down the driveway before I knew it. I pulled myself out of the seat and stood by the side of the car.

"Yeah, I'm going to be all right," I said, nodding my head.

I stood next to the car, looking around the property as Kenny got our bags from the trunk. He was doing everything for me; I just stood there, looking around. Our house and yard still looked beautifully manicured after two weeks without our attention. The grass was longer than I liked to keep it,

Love Notes 47

but I liked it that way some times. It looked more relaxed and full of life. The bird feeder had been snow white since I'd finally given in and painted it twice during the summer, like Marlena asked me. We had both worked together in the yard for hours on end. I painted the garage door while she painted the trim. I mowed the lawn while she edged. My jaw began to quiver and tears came to my eyes, but I shook it off before Kenny caught me. While she planted flowers, I would bring her fresh dirt in the wheel barrow. It was like a dance that we did together.

The big ceramic planters that we had got from her mother, sat next to the back porch stairs and looked like a professional floral arrangement from May until September. I walked up the stairs, past them, and headed for the door. As I put my key into the door, I felt that I was opening a page in history. I caught Kenny taking a quick glance at me. I noticed that he was looking at me every minute or two, I guess to see if I was okay. I tried to look like it was a normal day and I was coming home from the movies, not as though my heart were crying and my insides felt like wet cereal.

The house was quiet; not just free of noise, but lifeless. The sound of our shoes across the hardwood kitchen floor echoed for the first time that I had ever noticed. Everything felt different. The things that had always made me feel at home, in my place, with my belongings, now felt distant, like I was visiting a relative's home. Kenny had gone into the bedroom to put our bags away. As I looked around the kitchen, my eyes locked on the ceramic plaque the hung over the sink: *Marlena's Kitchen.*

I stood there staring at it as tears began to stream from my eyes.

"It is your kitchen, Baby. It will always be your kitchen," I said, unable to control myself. Within a few minutes, I felt Kenny's arm around my shoulders. He turned me around and walked me to the den, where I sat down and fell completely apart.

"Dad, let's go back to my house," he said. "It's probably still a bit too early."

"No, I'm alright," I said. "I knew this was going to be tough, but I'm alright." I went to the bathroom and splashed water on my face, hoping that would help me pull myself back together. After a few more deep breaths, I went back into the kitchen.

I had bought this corkboard with a calendar on it, which I hung on the wall next to the refrigerator. Once the kids had grown up, I had never wanted to see a refrigerator full of magnets, lunch menus, paintings, and report cards again, even though I loved it at the time. I glanced at the calendar. Tomorrow was the nineteenth. In that box she had marked Ceramics at 2:00 P.M. and duSable Museum at 3:30.

At that point I realized that I would have to start calling people who didn't know what had happened, like the people at the museum, and tell them that she couldn't help them with their senior group on Tuesdays and Thursdays anymore. My eyes were beginning to well when I heard Kenny walk into the room.

"You want a beer?" He said.

"No. Besides, I don't think you will want one either. It's domestic," I said.

Kenny smiled.

"I knew that it would be Bud or something, but I was going to suffer through it. You know. To be a good son."

We both chuckled mildly.

"Why don't you pour your old man a cognac," I said, feeling like a drink might be something that we could do together.

"Alright. I'll have one with you," he said.

"No suffering on the cognac. That's top shelf."

After he got the glasses and ice and left the kitchen for the den, I went back to the calendar. I mumbled to myself as I read the appointments on the calendar, and then froze when I noticed "WA" written with a black marker on the box for September 10. It was our little inside joke. "WA" was short for wedding anniversary, the date that we celebrate

Love Notes

with family and friends, but for Marlena and I, our real special day was what we called our Real Anniversary, the day that we had first met. I flipped the calendar back to June, where she had the sixth marked with two hearts. I let the calendar fall back to August. I listened for Kenny, but I didn't hear him. I walked into the den where I saw him sitting on the couch, staring straight ahead.

"I thought you were going to have a drink with me?" I asked him.

It didn't break the ice. He took a sip of his drink and continued looking ahead. I sat on the couch next to him and took a sip of my drink. This gave me a flashback of trying to get him to open up when he was a little kid and something was wrong. I sat patiently. After ten minutes of silence, he cleared his throat and spoke.

"I was home when you called me that morning, but I was in bed with some girl that I barely knew," he said in a self-defacing way.

"Kenny, that doesn't . . ."

"No. I was sleeping with some girl that I didn't even know when my mother died, and my father was trying to reach me. . . ."

"Kenny . . ."

"I didn't answer the phone because I thought that you may have been the girl that I've been seeing, calling to check up on me. So I didn't want to answer and have to talk to her with this other girl next to me. Pretty slick, huh?" He shook his head. I wanted to interrupt him, but I knew that it wasn't going to work. Kenny had to say what he had to say. "I wasn't there for my father or sister at the most crucial time in each of our lives, because I was playing college-boy player games. That's what was important to me: sleeping with one of my sister's friends, which will in turn cause problems for Kara, but hey, I wanted to get me some after Mom and Dad's party. I'm a young black attorney; I work out, have a nice car and condo. Look at me. I'm hot. I'm on fire. Try to put me out," he said as his voice began to crack. "You can't put me out. I'm too hot or too cold or maybe I'm too screwed up." Kenny tried to fight off the tears but they had taken over. He buried his head in his hands and let it out. It was a demon that was going to haunt him. I thought about how I could help him overcome this demon, when my mind went to where I thought Kara's demons would be. She and Marlena had their issues. They loved each other, but they were two very different women—old school and new school.

"Son, your mother knows that you love her. I know that you love me and would do anything for me that is humanly possible, so why are you beating yourself up because you didn't answer your phone for an hour?"

"Well, I guess it's not just that hour or whatever, but it's the fact that my life is a joke. I'm always going for it. Going for what? A nicer car? A bigger condo? What? It's a joke."

"Kenny, you and I both know that your life's not a joke. I think that it is unfortunate that tragedies such as this one make us aware of what is really important. I am not going to say for one minute that is why things happen, because I don't know. I don't believe that God needed to show us who's boss or to slap us to remind us of what is important. You will hear all of those things from well-meaning people over the next few weeks, but I want to tell you this: Listen only to what makes you stronger. You're a strong man, Kara's a strong woman, and we're a strong family."

Kenny hadn't let go and cried since the hospital. I put my hand on his back as he poured his heart out.

While I was walking out of the den toward the kitchen, I got this strange feeling, like I was being watched. I slowed my pace and then stopped once I got to the wall of family photos next to the door. There were black and white and color photographs of myself, Marlena, the kids, and other family members. I walked right past these pictures every day, but all of a sudden they were different. The people in each of the pictures were now looking at me with pity. I looked from one framed photograph to another. My aunt, my uncle, Kenny, Kara, Marlena, my grandmother, and grandfather all stared at me with the same sorrowful look. It was pitiful. I was pitiful. I nodded at my family and walked on.

I opened the refrigerator door out of habit; my eyes went to the wilting strawberries and the bottle of champagne. I shut the refrigerator door and opened the freezer. After I got the ice and returned to the den, Kenny had stopped crying and looked up at me through his reddened eyes. "How are *you* gonna make it through this, Dad?" he asked softly. "I've never told you this, but I have never met two people who were as close as you and Mom. Maybe that's why I don't take some of these girls seriously out here. When I compare them to Mom, they just don't stack up. Mom's friend, Mrs. Hunt, used to tell me that she didn't think that you or Mom could live a minute without each other."

The truth was that Mrs. Hunt was right, but now wasn't the time to tell him about that.

"She'll always be with me. I think that it's going to be strange, difficult, and lonely, but I am going to find a way. I don't know how yet, but I will find a way to continue to lead a fulfilling life. Maybe I will follow you around and see if I can keep you out of trouble."

"Well, you better get some real running shoes for that, not those eight-year old pair of Adidases I see you in sometimes."

A glimmer of a smile slipped from behind the clouds on his face.

Chapter 4

The first few days that I was home brought a new and unexpected challenge every hour. I didn't sleep the first night; I tossed and turned in the bed, often reaching for Marlena and finding nothing. I was tired but awake at 9 A.M., staring at the wilted roses on the nightstand, when the phone rang.

"Good morning. May I speak with Marlena, please?" The warm, elderly voice sang.

It was the little lady who Marlena drove to ceramics class. It was the first time that someone had called asking for her. I didn't know what to say.

"Who's calling?" I asked.

"This is Mrs. Lindsey. I was calling to see if Marlena can pick me up for ceramics from my sister's house on Forty-ninth Place instead of from my home." she asked cordially.

There was a silence on the line as I tried to figure out what to say. What do

I say? Sorry, she died nearly two weeks ago. No, she can't make it.

"Mrs. Lindsey, my wife won't be able to pick you up. She had an accident."

"Oh, no!" the Mary Poppins voice sang out. "Is she going to be alright?"

I took a deep breath. "She... uhh... no, Mrs. Lindsey. She's gone on," I said.

After nearly five minutes of "Dear Gods" and "Oh Jesus's", I got Mrs. Lindsey off the phone. After hanging up the phone, I stared at it for a minute. There would be many more calls like that and I would need to be ready for them. Not a minute had gone by when the phone rang again.

"Hello?"

"Mr. Brown?" the brash voice grated in my ear.

"Yes," I answered.

"This is Detective Rayborne. I've been trying to get hold of you to piece together some details on your wife's accident case. What I want to do is set a time when you can come in and we can talk," he said.

"Let me call you back in the next couple of days when I can . . ."

"Mr. Brown, every day that you wait is another day that puts us farther behind."

"I'll call you tomorrow," I said, before placing the phone back on the hook.

I hung up the phone and thought about sitting in a room with some cop, going over pictures of the accident, talking about the accident scene, and bringing all of that back into my mind. Marlena was gone and I needed a little more time to deal with that reality.

The smell of coffee had made it upstairs and into my nostrils. I was ready for a change of thoughts so I eagerly got up and went downstairs.

"Good morning," I said, walking into the kitchen.

"Hi, Dad," Kara responded, rising to greet me with a hug.

"Good morning," Kenny said.

"Dad, we're just having coffee and toast, but if you want something else, I would be glad to make it for you," Kara said.

"No, this is fine." I poured myself a cup of coffee, took a piece of toast, and sat down at the table and joined the kids in some small talk. I sat and listened, made a comment or two while my mind drifted back to my conversation this morning with Marlena's elderly friend, Mrs. Lindsey, and what I need to tell people who don't know what happened and how I would answer certain questions. *Are you married?* Yes. *How's your wife doing?* Great . . . I guess. *Can she drive to ceramics?* Not today. I don't know. I couldn't say that she was dead, because she wasn't dead. She wasn't walking around here gardening and fixing breakfast, but she wasn't dead; she had just passed on. This was going to be hard. As I sat, realizing that I couldn't solve that problem so easily, and hearing Kenny and Kara's talk as if they were a TV providing background noise, my mind drifted farther, taking me back to The Destiny Lounge on the south side, the night I first met Marlena. There was nothing on earth that compares to the second when I first laid my eyes on her.

Love Notes

"Dad?" Kenny's voice interrupted.

"Huh?" I looked over at he and Kara, and they were looking at me like I had missed something. "What?" I asked, looking back and forth between the two of them.

"Nothing. You just kind of went off somewhere," he said.

"I bet you were thinking about Mom, with that grin on your face," Kara tossed in. "Am I right?" she asked with a smile. I looked at the two of them.

"Okay. You might be on to something. I was thinking about her. I was thinking about when we met," I said.

"I've heard the story a dozen times from Mom, and you've just seemed to chime in when you were around, but I've never heard your version," Kara said, raising her eyebrows. Kenny gave me a shrug of the shoulders that said, "well?"

I took a few moments to search for words that could describe my feelings.

"Okay. When I first saw your mother, I knew. I knew in that second that she was going to be my wife. I was playing piano at The Destiny Lounge on the south side. We had a good crowd, which included four or five attractive young ladies who were sitting right in the front, but when your mother walked in, I never saw them or any other woman again. I mean, when I saw her, I couldn't take my eyes off her. As my eyes followed her around the room while she looked for a seat, I saw everything that I wanted in my life. I saw our house, you guys, a yard . . . everything right there."

"Was it a feeling or the way she looked or carried herself?" Kara asked.

"It was all of that. It was like when you know that something is right for someone who you know well? Like when you go to Kenny's condo, you know it's right for him. It fits him. This bracelet I bought you for Christmas last year," I said, lifting Kara's wrist. "Kenny was with me. I had been looking for a present for you for hours, and Kenny and I were going to give up for the day, when we passed the jewelry counter. I stopped and looked at the bracelet, then Kenny stopped and saw it and both of us said, "Kara." It's like that. I looked at

Marlena and said, "That's for me." I grinned and looked back and forth between the two of them.

"You guys need to get out of here; you're getting me all mushy," I said, blushing.

"Go on," Kara said.

"Well, once I came to grips with the fact that I was looking at my wife, I got scared. What if she looked at me and didn't see her husband? Or if she did, what if I said something stupid and made her change her mind?" I said.

"You got to be confident in your game," Kenny said. Kara and I both rolled our eyes at him.

"Actually you do have to be confident in your game, but there are people like your mother who can make you forget all about your game. When I first saw her, my game was gone. I sat playing, wondering what I was going to say or do to get her attention, when I thought about something that this brother had schooled me. Just a few days before I met her, this brother with this strong presence had come into the club. He was tall, dark, bald, and very smooth. I could tell that he was a musician. After we finished playing that night, he came up to the bandstand and told us who he was."

"Who was he?" Kenny asked.

"Did you ever hear of Dexter Gordon?"

"He was a horn player," Kara answered.

"Yeah. Dex was the man back then, and this brother who came in the club played bass for him. He told all of us in the band that we were good players, but to go to the next level, we had to make our instruments talk. He asked Charlie for his bass and gave us a little demonstration. His name was Blaine Carter. He took that bass and made that thing talk as clearly as I am talking to you now."

Kenny gave Kara a skeptical look. I raised my right hand as if I were taking an oath.

"I'm telling you." I put my left hand out like I was holding the neck of a bass and my right hand by my side, as if I were plucking the strings. "He told me to say something. I said, 'I like to groove' and he played it on the bass. *'I like to groove,'* " I said, trying to simulate the bass sounds. "He was bad," I said shaking my head. "The brother played piano too. He asked me to move aside for a minute while he showed me how it was done on the keys. 'Give me a few bars from the second to last song that you played tonight,' he said. I played a few bars from *Silk Dress,* and then he took over. He showed me how to make the song 'walk and talk,' as he said. Well, anyway, when I sat there playing in front of your mother for the first time, not knowing what to say if I got a chance to meet her, that was the first time that I truly made the piano talk."

"What?" Kara asked, smiling.

"The rest is history," I returned.

"No," Kara said. "Finish," she pleaded.

"We're here, aren't we?" Kenny asked.

Kara gave me a serious look.

"I played *Silk Dress* and *Swing Thing,* two songs that I had written with help from the band. But the way I made that piano sing and played looking into her eyes, she could see that I was playing for her. She was flirting with her eyes and I was flirting with my music. It was something else.

"When we finished playing, the people around her beckoned me to come down and talk to her. Everybody in the band was kidding me and making remarks like we were going to have to refund everybody else's money because I'd only been playing for one person that night. So I went down and talked to her. It was a little awkward at first, but you know how your mother makes people feel comfortable; after a few minutes, we were talking like we had known each other all of our lives. After I got comfortable, I did have to revert to a little game to get her number," I said.

Kenny took his fist and put it out to me. I made a fist and bumped his, like the young guys do. The kids looked fascinated. While taking a swig of my now-lukewarm coffee, I was startled by a sudden recollection of the old piano that was in the basement. I had forgotten all about it. I had stopped playing years ago, but I was anxious to know if I still had it. For some reason I wanted the kids out of the house so I could play with that piano and reminisce.

"Hey. I was just thinking, guys. I'm alright. Why don't you all get out of the house? Kenny. I know you have work at the office—go on in. Kara, you, too. I'll be all right for a few hours," I assured them.

After a bit of squabbling, I had them both out of the house in thirty minutes. As soon as they left, I raced down to the basement to uncover the piano. It was in the corner, covered with years' worth of junk. I removed the old army blankets, the Christmas decorations, the boxes of old books, and who knows what, until it was clear. I took an old towel and brushed off the dust from the piano and the bench. I probably hadn't played the thing in five years. I touched the keyboard with the same trepidation as a young boy kissing a girl for the first time. I pressed down on the "E" note and let it ring. Then I did an "E, F, G" three times and let that G ring and vibrate through my arm and into my body. It felt good.

I started with some scales and a few simple songs and after half an hour, I was playing old club songs and thinking that I was bad again. I started to play *Swing Thing,* a song that Johnny and I had put together back in the day. I like to say that it was the licks in that song that helped me land Marlena. It was a song that was fun to play. I must have spent an hour or so poking around at the keys before I was able to play it so it sounded like something. I was grooving on that middle part when I was startled.

"Dad!"

I looked around and Kenny was racing toward me, breathing heavily.

"Where have you been? I've been calling here since two," he said, catching his breath.

I felt like a child who had been caught red-handed and was about to get scolded.

"I was right here. I guess I didn't hear the phone," I said.

"Kara called and didn't get you, so she called me. We both tried most of the afternoon, before I decided to come over here to see if everything was okay."

"I'm fine. I just . . . uhhh . . . thought I might bang around on this thing and I guess I got a little carried away."

Kenny looked at me like he wasn't satisfied. I shut the key guard on the piano and stood up.

"What time is it?" I asked him.

"It's a little after seven."

I found it hard to believe, but I had been in the basement all day.

"Do you want to get something to eat?" I slipped in, changing the subject.

"Yeah, that'll be fine," he said. "Where do you want to go?"

"I have a taste for the fried green tomatoes at the Dixie Kitchen. What about you?"

"That sounds good. I've always liked their whole baby catfish."

Dinner was fine. I got Kenny to talk about his job and current events, and I got caught up to speed with a few of his friends. As we talked, I couldn't stop thinking about how good I had felt playing the piano. Playing brought me back to one of the best times of my life. This was my first good day since the accident.

When we got home, Kenny told me that he was going to go out for a while. He invited me, but I didn't want to go. Once he had driven off, I went straight to the basement.

I felt like I was being drawn to the piano. Since my earliest memories of my childhood, my mother had wanted me to become a pianist. I had long fingers for a kid my age and she thought that was the key to piano greatness. I couldn't have been older than five when I remember her working on my dad to buy a piano for me to play. I was seven when I took my first formal lesson. My father's reaction to being coerced into buying a piano was to make me practice for two hours a day, every day, with no exceptions. He had purchased that old piano from the Lively Stone Church choir for a hundred and twenty dollars. Making me play was his way of getting his money's worth. I hated it. I didn't like being forced to play as a way for my dad to get back at my mom for making him buy the piano, and I thought it was nerdy.

When I was sixteen, things changed. The day Typhani Taylor, the hottest girl in our high school, dropped the varsity quarterback to date a clarinet player from the school band, geeky band guys like me got cooler. Girls began to notice us, which made most of us play a little harder. As I got better, I began to play more contemporary music. In my senior year, I was in my first outside band. We played for parties, which got me hooked. The concept that I could hit the keys in a certain order and make people happy or sad was amazing. There was a song that we used to play called *Stroker* that never failed to make people jump up and dance. After hearing it in my head, I started to work on playing it. I missed a note or two here and there, and the piano was a bit out of tune, but after thirty minutes or so I had it. Marlena was never a big dancer, but I remember playing *Stroker* the second time that she came into the club and she got out of her seat and started moving. Once I learned how to really make the piano talk, I could bring people out of their seats to dance whenever I wanted, especially Marlena. The first time I saw her wear pants was this night at the club, when she had slipped in during the set, and I caught a glimpse of her as she was being seated. I was dying to get a better look at her in those pants before the end of my set so I decided that I had to make her get up and dance. I was playing *Stroker,* looking, staring, as I made the piano sing what I wanted her to do. Just like that brother from Dex's band had taught me, I had that piano singing: "Get up and dance, Baby, show those curves to me. Get up and dance, Baby, show those . . . "

"Dad!"

I looked back and found Kenny standing there looking at me with a disturbed look on his face. I stopped playing.

"Yeah?"

"Who were you talking to?"

"I wasn't talking," I said, looking at him with confusion. "Oh, I was singing a few lines from this music."

He looked at me as if I were wearing a dress.

"How was the club?" I asked him.

"It was cool. I went to this new place called The District."

"Oh, yeah?"

"Yeah."

"What kind of place is that?"

"It's a real contemporary loft-type club with comfortable seating downstairs and they have live upbeat kind of jazz upstairs."

"That sounds great. See anybody you knew there?"

"A few people, but uhh. . . . What play was this you were acting out?"

"I wasn't acting anything out, I was just singing a few of the lines. Anyway, I'm gonna turn in," I said, getting up from the piano and stretching my arms. He followed me up the stairs. I said goodnight and quickly disappeared into my room, where I joyously tossed and turned thinking about my wife, before falling into a deep sleep.

I thought the ringing phone was part of a dream, but by the third ring, I was awake enough to know that I had been in a deep sleep, but not awake enough to know where I was. I swung my arm out from under the covers and felt around the nightstand for the phone. I knocked the receiver off its cradle and then picked it up and pulled it to my ear.

"Hello?"

"Dad?"

"Yeah."

The sound of my daughter's voice in the middle of the night sent just enough adrenaline into my veins to wake me completely.

"Kara. How are you? Are you alright?"

"Dad, I'm sorry about waking you up. I . . ."

"No. Don't be silly."

"I was at home and I couldn't sleep and something just made me want to get out of there and go. I'm not too far away."

"Come on. You know you don't have to ask."

"I know. I just didn't want to startle you."

"Come on. I'll put on some coffee for me and some tea for you."

"That'll be great," she said with a hint of a smile in her voice. "I'll see you in a few minutes."

When I opened my front door, there stood my daughter, looking as weary as a war-torn soldier. I pulled her in by her arm and hugged her until it should have hurt. I continued to hug her while pushing the door shut when I noticed Kenny standing in the entrance to the living room. He nodded at me, shook his head, and turned around without Kara seeing him. I think he could see that she was probably going through what he had the night before and probably just wanted to spend time with her father. We drank coffee, reminisced, hugged, talked, and cried the night away.

When I woke up, both of them were gone. The phone rang a few times but I didn't answer. I just didn't feel like saying the same thing anymore:

> *I'll be okay. Yes, the whole thing is such a tragedy. We'll have to find a way to make it. Kenny and Kara are okay, but what can you expect? Yes, I was right there when it all happened. Yes, I have thought about counseling. I am looking at a few counselors now. No. I don't need anything. I think I'm okay for now.*

I wasn't in the mood for that today. I went into a kitchen drawer and got the household phone directory and located Reacco's number. Reacco is the son of one of Marlena's friends who does small construction projects. He's not the best, but he is easy to catch up with. I got him on the first try.

"Reacco."

"Yes."

"This is Hosea Brown."

"Hey, Mr. Brown. I heard about your wife. I'm sorry to hear about that."

"Thank you. Listen, Reacco. I have a project for you and I wanted to know if you are available any time soon."

Love Notes 77

"What is it?"

"I need you to enclose an area in my basement for me."

"Do I need to knock anything down?"

"No. I don't believe so. It's just for privacy."

"Okay. If you're gonna be home after five—no, let me make it five-thirty—I can take a look at it then."

"Okay."

"Yeah. Then I can give you a price and we can go from there."

"Great. I'll see you then."

For Reacco, five-thirty meant seven.

I spent the rest of the day at the piano, playing and replaying the songs that had brought Marlena and I together.

Reacco came at seven like I had expected. He looked at what I wanted and we agreed on a price.

"Mr. Brown, this job is right on time. Things have been slow at my job and my money has been real funny. I'm gonna knock this out tonight if I can."

"Tonight? It's seven-thirty now," I said. Reacco always underestimated the time it took him to complete a job, but this was ridiculous.

"Mr. B., it ain't nothing but two-by-fours, drywall, and a door. I'll be through by eleven-thirty."

I looked at my watch. Eleven-thirty meant two-thirty at best.

"It won't be no whole lot of noise either, because once I frame it out, I'm gonna use screws on the dry wall instead of nails."

"Alright, Reacco. Go ahead." I looked him in the eye, shook my head, and chuckled. He knew what I was laughing at.

"Naw . . . I'm serious, Mr. B., I'm gonna be cleaned up and through by twelve."

"Alright."

I reached into my pocket and peeled off the hundred and twenty dollars that he had estimated he needed for supplies.

"Reacco, I'm gonna leave the back door open, so when you get back, just come on in and get started. I haven't had a lot of sleep lately, so I may be in bed."

"Alright," he said, folding the money that I had given him and slipping it in his pocket.

* * *

It was seven o'clock when I woke up. The first thing I did was head for the basement. I looked out of the kitchen window before I went into the basement, because there was a chance that Reacco had fallen asleep downstairs.

I went to the basement with my curiosity piqued. When I got to the bottom of the stairs, there it was: a stark white cubicle in the middle of an otherwise dreary basement. I approached it like it was a UFO and walked the perimeter, examining the work. Some of the drywall seams didn't quite match up. There were a few spots where the screws had gone through, but he had done it. I opened and shut the door. It worked. I smiled, thinking about Reacco, who had probably just left. He had built a room in one evening. He could have had a good career as a carpenter with minimal training. I looked around the inside. It really wasn't bad. When I had gone to bed the night before, I was a bit concerned that Reacco might forget and leave the piano outside, which would have been quite a disaster because it wouldn't fit through the doorway, but he didn't. It was one of those times when Reacco was a good deal.

I went out and got the bench to the piano and brought it inside. I looked around the stark white room with the piano in the middle and it made me feel like I had when I was nineteen, moving into my first apartment. I dashed upstairs, looking for things to put in the room to warm it up. Within an hour I had five pictures of Marlena on the wall, an area rug that covered most of the floor, and an artificial rubber plant that I pulled out of the corner of the basement. The room was looking good. I sat looking at the pictures of Marlena and some of both of us when I realized that there was one thing that really belonged down there.

"The chest," I said out loud.

Chapter 5

I ran upstairs to the hallway where the pull-down stairs to the attic were. Marlena had made me promise that I would never go up into that attic when nobody was home. I looked up at the ceiling and apologized to her before pulling the rickety ladder down from the hall closet. We never put too many things up in the attic because of its difficult access. When I got to the top of the stairs, I saw the chest sitting in the middle of the floor. It was awkward to carry the bulky chest while trying to make it down the ladder-type stairs. Once I had made it down the stairs, my excitement was peaking about what might be in the old chest. After making it through the house and down to my piano room, I set the chest down on the piano bench and pulled up a chair. I looked down at the chest and then up at a smiling portrait of Marlena. I could see that she wanted me to open it.

I took a breath and lifted the creaky top. It was more packed than I had expected. There was a shoebox on the left, and about twenty or more dried roses neatly stacked in the middle. On the right were my cummerbund from the tuxedo I got married in, and the key from a broken piano that I had given to Marlena on one of our first dates.

I picked up the shoebox and opened it. It was full of letters. My heart flipped as I thumbed through what looked like every letter that I had ever written her, all in order of the dates that I sent them. There was a smaller gift-type box under the shoebox that contained little notes on everything from napkins to index cards to the backs of envelopes. I could feel the skin on my face stretching from my grin when I came to the original cocktail napkin on which Marlena had written her phone number. The napkin was browning and the writing was barely readable, but you could make it out. *Marlena Tucker, 726-5399.* I took the napkin and touched it to my lips. I looked up at Marlena's picture and dangled the napkin in front of it. "This was it. My last phone number in life." My grin was still fixed on my face, even though my eyes were starting to glisten.

The flowers were so frail that they disintegrated when I touched them, so I decided to leave them alone. I was able to distinguish a little white rose in the bunch. That was the flower that I had brought to Marlena's bedside right after she had given birth to Kara. "You kept that?" I said, looking up at her picture. I couldn't do anything but shake my head. "You are something else."

I rumbled around in the chest, before pulling out the cummerbund. From the tuxedo that I had worn at our wedding, it looked like a prop from a magic show. Marlena took it off me at our reception and told her girlfriends, *"The only thing that will ever be that tight around this man's waist again will be my arms."* I sat there thinking about the time she said that and how happy she was, surrounded by her girlfriends, happy about the wedding, and happy that she was married to me.

The black piano key ... I really couldn't believe that she had saved that. I used to talk so much smack back then. It must have been our second or third time seeing each other and as I was walking from the bus stop to her house, I came across a man at the top of an alley who was breaking an old piano apart with an ax to discard it. When he brought the ax down across the keyboard section, the keys exploded in all directions with a few of them landing by my feet. As I looked at the keys, I got what I thought was a brilliant idea. I picked up one of the black keys and stuck it in my back pocket.

When I got to Marlena's house, I told her that I had a special present for her. When I pulled the funny-looking key from behind my back, Marlena looked at it from two or three different angles and smiled at me. I handed it to her.

"It's for you."

"What is it?" she asked, giggling.

I smiled as I looked her into her eyes.

"You are holding the middle C from the piano that Ben Webster played at the Aargon Ballroom on New Year's Eve."

She rolled her eyes and let me into the house.

"What's more important, aside from being from Ben Webster's piano, is the fact that the middle *C* is what all the notes are built around. Without it, a piano won't make any sense. Without a center, nothing makes sense. I think I found my middle *C* when I met you," I said without losing contact with her eyes.

"Why don't you save some of that tall rap for later on when you know me? Besides, Mr. Hosea, I'm from the country so *I mights believe some of yo' charmin' tawk.*" With that she turned and walked away from me. I will never forget the sassy way that she waltzed out of the room. She looked back and smiled when she caught me with my eyes fixed a bit below her waist.

I set the piano key on the top of my piano and took a deep breath. I blinked away some tears before looking back into the chest. I looked at Marlena's picture before I reached for the box of letters. I opened the box, took out one of the letters, and held it in my hand. I then shut my eyes and thought about what was going on in our lives at that time.

Next thing I knew I was being awakened by a loud banging at the door.

"Dad, are you in there? Dad?"

It was Kenny. I glanced at my watch. It was 8:36.

"Yeah, Kenny. Just a minute," I said, trying to prepare myself for the impending situation. I rushed to the door and opened it and pushing myself out into the room.

"I guess I fell asleep," I said.

I pulled the door shut behind me and gave the knob a twist to make sure that it had locked.

"When did you put up this wall, or room, and for what?" he asked pointedly.

"Reacco just finished it yesterday."

"Why?" Kenny asked, looking behind me at the locked door.

"Well, I . . ."

"Why do you have a lock on it?" he asked. He looked both concerned and confused. I wasn't quite sure how to explain it to him.

"Well, I just wanted to have my little place where I go and work on my music and, I don't know. . . . I just wanted it to be private, for whatever reason."

"You've been spending all of your days and nights down here. You were asleep in there just now and you came up to the door and locked it as you came out. Don't you think that I should be concerned?" he asked.

"Yeah, I understand your concern, but I'm okay. Really. Playing the piano has been good for me. I guess it's my way of coping."

"That's fine, Dad. I can understand that, but the locking yourself in the basement part I don't."

I began walking toward the stairs as we talked, to keep him from asking me to let him in the room.

"I'll try to explain it to you a little later. Let me think on it, okay?"

"All right, but I want you to know that Kara and I are worrying about you more and more."

"I understand, and I appreciate it." I put an arm around him as we entered the kitchen. "Coffee?"

"Sure," he replied. "Dad, have you talked to the cops in the last week or so?"

"No, I . . ."

"Detective Rayborne called me and told me that he has been calling you and you haven't called him back. What's going on with that? I . . . I don't get it."

I looked away and then back at him as he stood staring into my eyes.

"Don't you want to see those guys who killed Mom go to jail?"

His words shot into me like arrows.

"Yeah, I want those guys put away. Of course I do."

"Well, why haven't you even tried to help the cops? You told us that you saw the guys who did it. I need for you to help me understand that. You have plenty of time to play around in the basement on the piano, but no time to help catch the guys who killed your wife? Help me out here."

Kenny's voice was piqued in anger and his comments sent my blood pressure through the roof. Angry blood raced through the vein in my neck and into my head. Part of me wanted to punch him in his mouth and another part of me wanted to collapse on the floor. We stood staring each other in the eye, man to man. I blinked.

"I'll call him in a few minutes," I said.

"Okay, great, but why haven't you tried before, Dad? Why? I want to see those guys hanging from a goddamn rope," he said, with his nostrils flaring.

Kenny never swore in front of me. He did it now to make a point of how angry he was. I could see that he wasn't going to stop without an explanation that he could accept. I bought some time by going to the stove and getting the coffee pot, then pouring more coffee into his cup and then into mine. He sat down on the edge of the chair and his eyes met mine when I was seated. I looked at him and looked away. I fidgeted with my hands and swallowed the lump in my throat before I began.

"Okay, I guess it seems like I'm not making a lot of sense to you lately. I understand how you might feel that way. I'm going to try to do my best to help you out. First things first: Why haven't I been at the police station or out on the streets, trying to find Mom's killers? Right. That's the first question, isn't it?"

"Yeah."

"Well, that's a good question. I think that I should be out there at the police station looking through mug shots and I should be out posting signs with a sketch of the killers. That's what *I* think that *I* should be doing, too, but I'm not. I think that I should be doing it. I'm disappointed in myself for not doing it. I don't understand why I don't want to do it." I shrugged my shoulders and shook my head. "I'm trying to hang on and deal with this thing the best that I can, but I'm just a shell." I took my fist and rapped it on my chest. "There's nothing in here. Everything's been sucked out— my strength, energy, heart, all gone. I'm here, but not really. So why am I not out avenging her death? I just don't have it right now. I know I need to get it, but I don't have it right now. That may sound like a pussy-foot lame answer, but it's all that I've got."

"Dad. I just was trying to . . ."

"Let me finish. About my 'playing around' in the basement with the piano, I probably don't have a great answer there either, but I'll try."

Kenny's rigid posture had softened. "Dad, I was just . . ."

I put my hand up.

"Let me finish. Every experience that I have known for more than half of my life, I have experienced with your mother. Think about that. From watching TV, gardening, and listening to music to going to church and eating. Her reactions were part of how I experienced things. I could tell by the look on her face when she ate something if I was going to like it, or if I heard her laughing in the other room, I would run in there to watch TV, because there was a funny show on. I tried to watch TV the other day, and now I don't know whether I like something or not. When I look at anything, it's like I am looking at it with one eye: I don't have that other perspective that I have always had, so it's awkward. Everything is awkward, so playing around in my room down there is the only thing that gives me any sort of good feeling. I don't know what it is, but all I can say is that it makes me feel better, and I think getting better is what I need to be doing. Maybe it's some sort of survival mode. I don't know." My head dropped on its own when I finished. I lifted it up and my eyes met Kenny's and we looked each other in the eye for a moment and then away.

"Well, how are you feeling physically?" he asked me.

"Not real bad. I'm making it. Falling asleep like I did last night at the piano is good. I like looking up and it's morning. It's a painless way of getting to the next day. Catching those guys is important. It really is very important to me. I just haven't been able to do it."

"Would it help if I went with you?" Kenny asked gently.

"Yeah, I think it would. I could probably use the moral support. What about you? You told me that you've been having dreams about catching and killing the guys who did it. Is that right?"

Kenny chuckled.

"Yeah. Last night, I dreamed that I was in a bar and I overheard two guys talking about a car they hit and ran away from in a park. I then took a bar stool and cracked them over their heads and proceeded to beat them until I was restrained by four or five guys."

"What do you make of these dreams?" I asked him.

"That I'm angry?"

"Yeah, I would say that, but I think that you could also conclude that these dreams illustrate your need to do something about this. Everybody needs to find a way of coping, and maybe yours is to get involved in this case with the police, and help solve this crime."

Kenny wagged his head from side to side, evaluating what I had just told him.

"Maybe. I really hadn't given it much thought." He shrugged his shoulders and studied my eyes. "I probably need to get back to the office," he said, standing up. "I will set up a meeting for us and the detective to talk, and I will give some thought to getting more involved."

"Okay."

He looked at his watch and then at the clock on the stove. "Talk to you later," he said as he dashed out the back door.

I watched him walk to his car through the window over the kitchen sink, like I had when he was a kid going to school. It was clear to me that burying himself into this case and working with the cops would be good for him. His sense of fairness and justice wouldn't allow him to sleep well until this thing was solved. As Kenny drove away, my concerns turned to Kara. I began to wonder what she would need to do to help her deal with what had happened. The more I thought about it, the more I wanted to know. I put in a call to her to try to set up dinner.

Even though Kenny's words had made me take notice of the things in my life that weren't getting done, I still found myself descending the stairs to the basement, to my little room. Those letters in the chest were eating at me.

As I reached the last few stairs and looked at the newly built room in the middle of an otherwise dreary basement, I understood why it aroused such curiosity and concern. I stood outside the room and wondered if perhaps I were actually out in left field and didn't know it.

The key to the room wasn't on my big key ring: I kept it on a metal beaded chain of its own. For a second, when I slipped the key into the lock, I got the feeling that you get when you have finally made it home after a long day. I opened the door and locked it behind me.

Everything was just as I had left it. The black piano key sat on top of the piano. A few flaky remnants of the old roses were laying on the area rug beneath the piano seat where the chest sat. I sat down on the folding chair and ran my eyes over the wooden chest. To me it was as much of a treasure chest as any. I looked at my watch. It was 12:15 P.M.. I wanted to keep track of time so I could be ready for dinner when Kara called.

I opened the chest and looked over its contents before deciding to go for the cigar box full of notes. I flipped open the top of the box and pulled out a wrinkly old bar napkin. My face burst into a smile when I saw what it was.

> *If you wink at me two times and smile, I will play that Fats song for you or you can blow me a kiss, and I'll play the rest of the night dancing like Little Richard.*
> *Hosea*

I remembered laughing to myself when I wrote the note because I thought that I had created a win-win situation for myself. I spent the night watching her, looking for my two winks and a smile or a beautifully blown kiss, but instead at ten-thirty she got up, smiled at me, and left. I was hot. She was playing with me and it drove me crazy. I wanted to call her when I got off work at one, except she lived with her mother and I didn't dare call at that hour. I could tell that she took joy in messing with me because of the smile that she flashed me when she walked out of the club. I called her at eight the next morning.

"Hello?"

It was her. It sounded like she had been up, had juice, coffee, and a full breakfast.

"Miss Hansen, you're wrong."

"Is that you, Mr. Hosea Brown?"

"Yeah, it's me."

"I'm wrong? It's eight-o-one in the A.M. and I don't think that I've been up long enough to do anything that wrong," she said.

"You know I was a hundred percent fixated on you last night, waiting for you to choose A or B, and you just left me hanging."

"Well, that's funny. I was feeling like you left me hanging," she shot back.

"How did I leave you hanging?"

"Well, so far you have been such a clever and resourceful man that I was sure that you were going to come up with more choices than just your A and B. I was thinking that you might give me an option C or D, you know, something a little more daring," she said, taunting me, knowing that we both knew that she was more conservative than I was.

I refolded that little bar napkin and gently placed it in the box. That felt good, I thought. I figured that reading that note would seem like an appetizer, compared to reading the letters. I took the top off the shoebox and reached in and took the first letter from the stack. These were the letters that I had written to her after our short breakup, near the beginning of our relationship. I looked at the envelope: *Marlena Hansen* with her mother's address on the south side, and then I flipped it over to the back. The return address was my first apartment over on Prairie Avenue.

I remembered sitting in one of those rickety old kitchen chairs, writing that letter, and then carefully printing the envelope. I looked through the tattered opening at the top of the envelope to the folded sheet of paper with ink bleeding through it. I pulled the letter out and looked at it. I never understood it and still don't. Marlena broke up with me the day I was headed to her house to tell her that I knew that I wanted to spend

Love Notes

my every breathing moment with her. I knew that we had only been together for a few weeks, but I thought she felt the same way that I did. I wasn't proposing; I just wanted her to know how I felt. She was stern and cold in a way I hadn't thought possible when she told me that she thought that it would be best if we ended things then and there. I had never felt more confused and deflated in my entire life. I couldn't accept that it was real, because I had felt so sure that I knew what was in her heart.

I looked at the date on the envelope. The faded postmark read July 25, 1966. I pulled the letter out and looked it up and down. In the upper right hand corner, I had printed the date and time. It read July 25, 11:48 P.M., which sent my mind back to the kitchen table of that apartment where I had written the letter.

I had spent the entire day trying to put onto paper what was in my heart and on my mind. At eleven forty-eight, I finally had it.

Marlena, July 25 at 11:48 P.M.

When you read these words, I want you to hear them as if they are coming from my lips. I want you to see me looking into your eyes the way I did the first time I said, "I love you."

You asked me to respect your decision to break up . . . it's hard. What you told me, I can't understand. You told me that you are just a simple girl and may not be worldly enough? I may seem complex, but I am simple as well. I have always wanted someone who I can love, adore, and share every wonderful thing in this world with. I love you for every thing that is you. I love your mannerisms, like the way your smile goes down, then up. I love how you blink your eyes. I love the way you look at me. I love everything about you.

Every waking moment of every day and every piece of every dream is about you. When I shut my eyes, I see you as if you are right in front of me, but when I open my eyes and the dream is gone, it hurts.

Love Notes 101

Since you've been gone, I think about being with you and holding you from sun up to sun down. Even while I write this letter, my mind takes me back to how wonderful it was to hold your hand, feel your lips, or how I felt when I looked at you and knew you were mine.

When I fell in love with you, I gave you my heart . . . it's yours forever.

I will love you every day that I am on earth and into eternity.

Hosea

I put the letter down and thought about how this letter that I had written over thirty-five years ago so accurately described how I felt at the time. Everything was gray. What were probably the most beautifully rich, velvety red roses next to our house might as well have been dandelions, and the sky was the color of charcoal. I reviewed the letter again and set it on the music holder of the piano. As I sat staring at the letter, a part of the letter jumped out at me, *"living without a heart."*

I took another look at Marlena's portrait above the piano and shut my eyes and visualized being with her. I saw the two of us walking along the lake, working in the back yard, playing Scrabble on the den floor. While my mind drew a picture of her pruning roses in the garden, I began to hear music. At first, the music seemed normal, not appropriate for a daydream, but it wasn't just in my mind: This music was real. When I opened my eyes, I lost the vision of Marlena, but the music played on. It was slow piano jazz, with individual notes that floated from the sky like a ballet of snowflakes on a winter night.

Chapter 6

My hands had been simply resting on the keys of the piano, but when I looked down, they were moving. Like watching the keys move on a player piano, I watched my hands play the music that was coming from overhead. I felt like I was in a trance or in a different dimension. I couldn't tell whether I was playing what I was hearing or whether my hands were acting on their own. I wanted to capture what was happening, experience it again, but what was happening was happening and I couldn't imagine trying to stop it. Where was Kenny barging in to see how I was doing? I thought to myself how I wanted someone else to see and hear what was happening. I was playing, listening, and somehow participating in what was the most beautiful, heart-moving music that I had ever heard. I wanted to hold onto a piece of it and not let it slip away. I wanted to record it. I had a tape recorder upstairs in my bedroom, but I was scared to leave out of fear that whatever was happening would never happen again. As I let the music play through me, I began to feel comfortable with it, like I knew it and trusted that it wasn't just going to go away. I pulled my hands away from the piano and paused. I put them back on the keys and my hands began playing again. I smiled as if I were playing a game with someone. I took my hands off the keys again and calmly stood up, walked to the door, and then took off running up the stairs to get my tape recorder. I scaled the stairs two at a time, darted through the kitchen, and into the den, where I remembered that there was a smaller cassette recorder in the closet. I ripped the small cassette player off the shelf, sending a few board games crashing to the floor. As I dashed through the kitchen, I noticed the red light was flashing on my answering machine, but I kept going. I raced until I got to the door of the piano room and then I slowed down before going inside. I put the recorder on top of the piano and rewound the cassette that was inside. As the cassette rewound, I sat trying to catch my breath. I looked around the room as if I were going to see musical notes coming out of the sky. I didn't see any notes, but I could feel them. It was still there, I said to myself as I smiled.

I turned the recorder on and tried to calm myself for a few seconds before placing my hands on the keyboard. Within seconds, it was happening like before. The music was coming and my hands were playing. I looked up at the tape recorder and it was running.

When the tape stopped after thirty minutes, I flipped it over and started to hit the record button, but instead I remembered the flashing light on my answering machine upstairs. It could have been Kara. I thought about stopping to check it out, but my hands went back to playing. I played for about fifteen more minutes, when the music trailed off. I looked around, shut my eyes, and listened, but it was gone. The room was silent. I sat there, breathing heavily, amazed at what had transpired, when a disturbing thought jumped into my mind, causing my body to tense. I wondered if I had somehow been dreaming all of this, when I heard the soft brushing sound of the cassette player's motor turning. I hit the stop button and then rewound the tape.

After poking the play button, I felt a smile grow on my face when I heard the music coming from the tape recorder. As the music played, I looked up at Marlena's picture and then at the letter I had been reading when the music started. I took the letter from the music holder, looked at it, and folded it before putting it back in its envelope. I held the envelope between the thumbs and forefingers of both hands and rubbed back and forth with my eyes shut trying to put some meaning to what was going on.

I placed the letter back inside the shoebox and pulled out the next one. The postmark on the second letter read July twenty-seventh, just two days after the first. I was becoming antsy about checking the answering machine to see if it was Kara who had called, but I had to take a look at the second letter.

Seeing the stationery took me back to my feelings when I wrote it. I was trying not to mope, but I was numb. I was wallowing, trying to keep my chin up and have faith that my first letter made her change her mind, but I wrote the second one just in case. I remember racing upstairs to my neighbor's apartment to borrow what I was certain would be beautiful stationery. It was stationery and it was nice paper, but it was simply a plain, cream-colored bond. I took it down to my apartment, set it on the table, and wrote at least fifteen drafts before I was ready to put my chosen words on the stationery. Just as I was about to write the first words on the paper, I got what I thought was an excellent way to jazz up the stationery. I had a bouquet of roses that I had bought and stuck in the refrigerator after deciding against putting them on Marlena's doorstep. I took one of the roses and held it over a pan of boiling water so it would get warm and collect steam. I pressed it onto the paper as hard as I could with a book.

When I lifted the rose from the paper, it had left a beautiful impression on the paper, which added just the right amount of color to it. I remember thinking that she would probably think that I had gone out and bought it from some fancy department store. Once the paper had dried, I carefully transcribed the letter from the notebook paper onto the stationery. I was proud of what I had done when I licked the flap to seal the letter.

Marlena:
I walk around my apartment with your picture in my hand, staring at it and talking to it as if it's you. I told you I loved you perhaps a hundred times. I dropped to my knees and asked God to bring you back.

Even though I look at the clock and it barely moves and I look at the phone and it never rings, I have faith that he will bring you back to me. Some things in life are inevitable, and we are powerless to control them. The sun will rise, the birds will sing, winter will change to spring, and you and I will be together.

I bought a dozen roses that I was going to bring to your house and lay by your doorstep, but it was too hard for me to go to your home knowing that I am so close to you, yet so far away. Instead I sat in my living room and took the flowers and played "She loves me, she loves me not," and every time it came up, "she loves me."

The last rose that I came to was bigger and more beautiful than the rest. It's the one on top of this letter. I steamed it and pressed it onto this paper. It's not the real rose, but a good impression. Like your picture, it's not you, but it's what I have to live with for now.

When we met, I felt that it was God's will. It's his will and I believe that through all of this, he will find a way. Knowing that, it's still hard to be patient. For now, I cherish every thought and memory of you that rises from the depths of my heart and soul.

Love eternally,
Hosea

After we got back together, she told me that she wasn't able to sleep after she got this letter, thinking about how she was going to cope when she knew in her heart that I was the one and no one else would do.

I looked at the smudge, the rose impression, and then up at her photo; she was the one and no one else will ever do. I pulled myself together and headed upstairs.

The first message on the answering machine was from Kenny, letting me know that we had an appointment with Officer Rayborne at ten o'clock the next day. The next message was from Kara,

Love Notes

telling me she could meet me for dinner at a place called Snaps at seven-thirty. I looked at the clock and it was twenty after six. I hadn't showered or shaved, nor did I even know where Snaps was.

I arrived at the restaurant at seven-twenty-five, certain that Kara would have been waiting for at least ten minutes because she was always early. The place was small enough for me to see the whole dining area, but I didn't see her.

"I can show you to a seat while you wait for your party," the hostess said.

"No, thanks, I'd rather wait here," I told her.

I sat and looked around as I settled down after all my hustling to get there. The décor was contemporary, but warm. Marlena would have liked it. Kara had probably chosen it because of the Creole cuisine, which she knew I would like.

"Hi, Dad," she said as she walked through the doorway. I stood up and gave her a hug.

I kissed her on the head. "How are you, Ginger?" I used to call her Ginger when she was little. I still call her that occasionally, especially when it's just the two of us.

After the waiter had taken our orders and we had run through some perfunctory small talk, Kara curbed her conversation to give me an opportunity to share with her whatever it was that had invoked this urgent meeting. I thought that I was ready. I reached across the table and covered her hand with mine.

"Honey, I hope I didn't alarm you with the message that I left. Did I?"

She tipped her head to the side. "Well, I don't think that you've ever called me with that kind of urgency before, so . . . I was a little concerned."

"I'm sorry about that. There is no 'big issue' or problem. Not really," I said sheepishly. "This morning I realized that I have been working hard on healing myself and finding a new way of living, and I felt like I haven't been attentive enough to what may be going on with you."

I squeezed her hand and she squeezed mine back.

Love Notes 113

"The 'emergency' is that I got a gut feeling that some things are going on with you and you have needed me in the last couple of days. I may be off base, but that's it." She batted her eyes and smiled at that. "There was a situation a long time ago when me, you, and your mother were having dinner. You must have been twelve or thirteen years old and Kenny was at the Pony League field at practice when your mom jumped up and told me to stop and go to the field and see about Kenny. All she said is that she felt that something was wrong."

"Yeah, I remember that. I think we were having pork chops and you were not trying to leave a plate of Mom's pork chops to go anywhere."

We both started laughing.

"I wasn't trying to leave Marlena's pork chops to do anything. But anyway, I went and sure enough, when I got there, some older guys from the west side were over there trying to take their equipment."

"Yeah, I remember that, " she said.

"My panicking about seeing you today is one of those kind of parent things. Am I right? "

As I looked at her, I could see a perfect reflection of the candle on our table flickering in her eyes, which were starting to well up with tears.

"I spent most of my life being mad at Mom, because she somehow knew what was happening or about to happen in my life. I used to tell her that she was wrong and too old to know what was going on.... " Identical tears sprouted from the corners of her eyes and raced down her cheeks, making a small splat when they hit the tablecloth.

"I didn't speak to her for almost two months and told her that she didn't understand anything but being in the kitchen. I told her she didn't want me to be happy when she told me not to go out with that guy Tony, who turned out to be racist and everything else she warned me about."

I gripped her hand tighter. I looked away for a moment while I searched my mind for something to make her feel better.

"Your mother understood and she admired you more than you think she did. I always shook my head at the two of you. You two are more alike than either of you realized. You're both so organized and capable of coordinating things and pulling things together. Now, granted, she was doing them for the household and for her community work, and you organize and put things together in business, but it's the same. Somehow you two couldn't get over the contemporary woman versus old-fashioned woman thing. I think that if Marlena had been born when you were, or you had been born when she was, you two would be the same."

There was a long silence as we both pondered what I had said.

"Yeah, I would like to believe that I would have been as smart and intuitive as she was if I had been born at that time, but I don't know. You were right, though; there has been a lot going on with me. I feel like my whole focus has been totally wrong. This whole career thing—what am I doing? Or trying to do?"

Just then the waiter interrupted. "The snapper for the lady and the jerk Cornish hen for the gentleman. Will there be anything else?"

We both shook our heads and stared at the beautiful-looking food with little interest. I didn't have any appetite and I could see that Kara wasn't going to eat much either. We both reached for our wineglasses at the same time. I tapped her glass with mine, before we took our sips.

Kara took out a tissue and patted the tears from around her eyes.

"What are you saying about your career?"

"None of it makes sense anymore. As much as I used to insinuate to Mom that being a homemaker was old-fashioned and somehow unsophisticated, I'm thirty-four-years old. When Mom was my age she had a home, two children and a husband who worshiped the ground she walked on. That's what every woman wants on the inside. What do I have?"

"Honey, you've got everything. You've got . . ."

"Nothing," she said, finishing my sentence.

The flow of tears from her eyes resumed. "I've got nothing. Nothing. Oh, yeah, I forgot. I've got an MBA, a loft, a BMW, and a membership at the Lakeshore Athletic Club. Yeah, great."

I could feel the tears forming in the back of my eyes, but I didn't want to let them out. If Kara saw tears in my eyes, she would immediately feel bad for making me upset and then close up. It has always been very painful for me to see her hurting. I remember standing outside her hospital room when she was thirteen and crying when the doctor was giving her stitches. But now, as with Kenny, I had to be quiet and listen to her as she suffered through her demons, as I called them.

"Dad, right now, I'm questioning my whole life. It's like I'm really trying to be something or prove something to someone, but who? Who cares if I can run ten miles, or that I have these *things,* or that I am this senior buyer for Nordstrom's. Those things don't do anything for you when you're hurting inside, you're lonely, and you need someone who cares about you."

I slid my free hand under the table and balled it up in a fist, trying to relieve some of my frustration at not being able to do anything to help my baby girl.

"In the last week and a half, I feel like everywhere I look there's someone with a newborn baby. Or little kids will run up to me and look at me, like there's something wrong with me. It's like they look at me and they know how I feel on the inside."

"Is there something wrong with the dinner?" the waiter interrupted.

Kara and I looked at the untouched food.

"No. It looks great; it's just that we've been talking. I don't think that we are going to eat any of it." I looked at Kara, who gave me a quick nod. "Can you wrap it up?" I said.

"Not a problem." We sat silently as he removed the untouched entrees. I thought about what was happening to her. As I had suspected, she was having a tough time. God was talking to her, but I decided to wait until I found the passage in the Bible before I shared it with her. I talked her into spending the night at the house, because I knew that she needed me.

It seemed that each of us had said so much at dinner that we didn't have a lot to say for the rest of the evening, but I think that it was very comforting for both of us to know that the other one was there.

Chapter 7

Kenny and I pulled up outside the police station at 9:55 A.M.. By 10:10, we were at Officer Raymore's desk, well into his questioning. When the overweight detective pulled out a folder full of photographs of the accident scene, Kenny reviewed them before passing them on to me. He and Officer Rayborne seemed to be bonding as the detective showed him the strategy and progress of the investigation. After looking at photographs of the truck, which turned out to be a Lincoln Navigator, the officer began to show me mug shots of possible suspects. I looked at photo after photo of young black men for what seemed like an hour, until they all began to look the same.

"Mr. Brown, I can see you're getting a bit tired here. Let's try this again another day," he said, pulling one of the big mug-shot books toward him. "But before we call it quits, there is one little detail that I need you to help me clear up." The detective pulled out a cardboard panel, which had a stenciled diagram of the accident scene on it. "Mr. Brown, you told me that you saw the two perpetrators exit the truck from the driver's door, and one of them dropped something metallic looking?"

"Yeah."

"Okay. Please stop me if I am wrong," he said, pointing to the diagram with an ink pen.

"You were driving behind your wife when you saw headlights move from left to right into your lane."

"Yes."

"And your wife, who was ahead of you, veered slightly to the right?"

"Yeah."

"Then the vehicle struck her car and pushed it into this tree over here."

Those words hurt.

"Yeah."

"Then you came to a stop right here."

"Yeah."

"You got out of the car and went to your wife's car door, couldn't get it open, went back to your car, got your spare key, and opened her door."

I nodded and looked over at Kenny, who was studying the officer intensely.

"The paramedics say that they found you right here, next to your wife." He poked the cardboard mock-up right next to Marlena's driver's side door.

"Alright."

"So the accident happens, you're right there, you stop here, you get out, go to the car, can't get in, you get your key, go to the car, open the door, your wife's body falls out, you fall onto the ground, and according to the paramedics, right here is where they found you, next to your wife."

"Yeah."

"They revived you on the way to the hospital."

Kenny and I looked at each other and shrugged our shoulders.

"Alright."

"Bear with me one more second," he said. "Okay, if that is the way it happened, then how could you possibly have seen these guys get out of the car and drop something when you were here on the right side of the truck, and they were clear on the other side? From where you were lying, here, you couldn't have seen them through the window. You see my problem?" He set the cardboard diagram in a chair so we could all see it and turned and looked at me, breathing heavily through his nostrils. I looked at him and back at the diagram. Kenny studied the diagram and then turned and looked at me as well. The officer grabbed his dirty coffee mug and brought it to his mouth and took a swig.

I had an explanation, but I wasn't ready to discuss the time I spent out of my body and all of the ramifications that that would bring. I was cornered.

"What are you saying? That I'm making this up and going through hundreds of mug shots until I find a guy who I want to hang for my wife's death? What are you saying? Huh?" I stood up abruptly. Kenny stood up as well. The detective remained seated.

"Dad, I don't think that the detective was trying to say anything. I think he was just trying to understand."

"Trying to understand? Understand what? Why I decided to come in here and make up a big story on how I saw my wife's killers, when I didn't? Let's get out of here," I said to Kenny, as I turned toward the door.

I looked back to see Kenny shaking hands with the detective and giving him his business card. I felt bad, cornered, and more than anything else, dishonest, but I didn't know what to do. The detective was doing what detectives do, but I wasn't ready for it. Detective Rayborne was like a real-life Colombo who had one detail that he couldn't quite figure out—something that I hadn't considered. What was I supposed to say: "I see how you could be confused, Detective, normally I couldn't have seen what was going on, except that during those four to seven minutes that the paramedics estimate that I was dead, I had a little 'out-of-body' experience that put me above the whole accident scene so I could see better?"

I heard Kenny's footsteps racing across the linoleum floor, trying to catch up with me. Once he had caught up to me, he didn't say anything. We walked to the car, got in, and had a silent ride home. Both of us wanted to say something, but we didn't. I knew my son, the lawyer, was dying to grill me about my strange behavior.

When we pulled up at the house, Kara's car was still there. Kenny drove up the driveway and left the engine running.

"I've got to be at a meeting at one, so I need to get going," he said.

"Okay."

We both paused.

"Is Kara alright?"

"Yeah. We had dinner last night and she decided to spend the evening over here. She's going through it like all of us, but in her own way."

"Oh. Like you were telling me that maybe the Lord wants me to help solve this crime since I was dreaming about getting the guys who did it? For healing?"

I took a moment to determine if Kenny's comment was sarcastic.

"Yeah, partially. And the other part is just normal pain from the situation."

"Yeah," he said softly. He looked at his watch. "I wish I could come in, but I have to get out of here. Tell Kara that I'll give her a call this afternoon."

I nodded. I stepped out of the car and watched him drive away. I stood in the driveway for the next few minutes, thinking about how defensive I had become, trying to hide the strange little things that were happening and that I didn't want to talk about. I wondered if it might be better to just tell him what had happened and let him think I was off my rocker, rather than grumpy. It was time that I told him and Kara everything.

* * *

I walked into the house half-expecting to smell food cooking. I don't know why. I know Kara probably didn't cook for herself, but she is a great cook when she wants to be. Instead it was quiet, perfectly quiet. There was no scent of cooking foods, no coffee smell, no radio, no TV, nothing. I walked cautiously through the kitchen. I peeked into the den and walked down the hall to the bedrooms.

"Kara?"

I picked up my pace as I looked for her. I checked the bathrooms, looked behind doors and into closets.

"Kara?"

I looked outside at her car again. It hadn't moved.

"Kara!"

I then went back into the guest bedroom to check for her things. Her purse was next to the bed, standing open, so I was able to see her wallet and keys. As I walked to the hall closet to check for her coat, I thought about the basement. Kara never went down in the basement, but it was the only room left. I dashed around the corner to the basement stairs.

"Kara?"

The light was off. I turned it on and walked down the stairs. When I got to the bottom, I saw the door to my piano room was open, and it seemed like there was a glimmer of light inside. I paused, and then approached it slowly.

My insides got heavy. With every step, a new wave of a bad "what-if" ran across my mind. When I got to within four feet of the door, I could see her body hunched over the piano, her thick mane of hair covering her face and neck. My stomach turned to lead. As I stood frozen in the doorway, she lifted her head and looked at me with her face awash in tears. Her tear-swollen eyes were wide, like those of a deer caught in a car's headlights. She uttered no words, but I heard her loud and clear: *"Daddy, I am hurting. Help me."*

I rushed to her side and took her in my arms.

"I'm sorry," she said through the tears.

"I . . . Kenny had told me that you had this room and I . . ."

"Shhhh. Don't say anything. I'm here for you."

As I held her, I took a quick glance around the room, looking for what she might have seen that was so painful. There was the single black piano key lying on top of the piano; the Bible.

Then I glanced over her shoulder to the other side of the bench and saw the shoebox of letters from the chest, open and half full.

"The letters!" I screamed to myself.

There were three letters on the music holder on top of the piano, one on the floor, and there were several lying open in the chest. Her teary voice rose from my left shoulder, where her head rested.

"I'm sorry, Dad. Kenny has been telling me about this room and how you were spending your days in here and I just wanted to see it and . . ."

"It's okay."

"I was able to use a credit card on the door, like Kenny and I did when we were kids, and get in, but I just wanted to see, and then I saw the box and when I read one letter. . . . "

"It's okay, honey. Really. It's okay. Did you read a lot of them?"

"Yeah, I read them all. I have never seen anything so beautiful. I just couldn't stop. I couldn't stop imagining you and Mom back when those black-and-white pictures were taken, in your twenties, madly in love with each other. I felt like I could really see it," she said, lifting her head from my shoulder. I rubbed her hair, thinking about what she had said. *She could see us back during that time.* Was it the letters? The things in the room? Or was it something else, something that she was supposed to see?

"That's what I do down here—just what you were doing," I said, taking a seat next to her on the piano bench. "But I don't cry. Well, I try not to. I smile. I laugh. I daydream. I reminisce, and I play music. Music that comes to me when I think about your mother and all of the things that are us," I told her.

I heard a sniffle, and turned to look at her face, where she had formed the hint of a smile.

"This little room, my cave, whatever you want to call it, has been my salvation in many ways. I don't know why I needed to build it or why I wanted it private, but I did. I am really glad you did discover it, because I think it's helping you understand where I am emotionally.

I'm different, and I think I am changed forever. I know that I have needed to share a few unique experiences that I have had with you and Kenny, but I've been afraid. I know that Kenny has probably called you and told you that I'm acting strangely. I'm sure you guys are wondering if I'm in shock. I know that you two have probably discussed what to do if I've really lost my mind."

She chuckled at that.

"See? I know you guys have probably already found me a home where I can get help, but I'm all right. At least I think I am. I see things in a new way, a good new way. Remember that day when I first came home and you and Kenny were looking at me in the kitchen smiling, and you told me that I must be thinking about Mom?"

"Yeah."

"Then I told you the story again about the first day that we met? Well, let me tell you a little secret. When I told you and Kenny that you guys should go to work, I wanted the house alone. As soon as you two left, I ran downstairs and uncovered this old piano and stared at it. While I sat on it thinking about how I used to play it for Marlena, my hands just started to move. When you told me how you could see me and Mom in our early days, just from sitting here reading the letters, that first day, when I touched that first key, it propelled me back to that club where we met, like it was happening in real time. And it has been like that ever since. When I play, I'm telling you it's like I go right back there. I'm looking at her, making eyes at her, showing off for her. It's unexplainable. I started to feel weird when Kenny would walk in and I am in the middle of a flashback, singing or talking or playing the piano. I think that's why I built the walls.

"What's in here isn't a secret; it's just that I wanted to spend time in here by myself enjoying what was happening and at the same time trying to figure it out. It was like I was drawn down here to the piano, but it's more than the piano. It's weird, but once the room was built, I walked inside and I was like, "this is it." It sounds crazy, huh?"

Kara shook her head. "No. It's not crazy. It's . . . I wish, I wish that they still made guys like you, who love their women like you love Mom, and I wish that I could meet one of them."

She leaned over and gave me a big hug, which I needed.

"Thanks," I told her.

We both sat for a few moments in silence. I sat thinking about the sadness in Kara's eyes, but more so the softness and vulnerability that I hadn't seen since she was a little girl. I looked at her and I wondered what was on her mind.

"A Tootsie Roll for your thoughts," I said.

She got up and pulled the piano bench in front of me and sat down and looked me in the eyes.

"You're right. Kenny and I have been worried about you, wondering if you were in shock or depressed, and we have talked about what, if anything, we could do about it. But I don't feel that way anymore. Ahh . . ."

"Go ahead."

"Okay. You told me that it's okay that I read the letters. Right?" she questioned, raising her eyebrows, and gesturing.

"Yeah."

"Well. . . ."

"Well, what?" I said.

"What happened?"

"Oh. You mean, what happened. Why did she leave?"

"Yeah."

I took a deep breath and shook my head.

"I don't know. I've never known."

"I mean, you guys meet, fall in love, and then . . ." She shook her head in confusion.

"It was out of the clear blue. I went to her house and everything was going great, but when she came to the door, I knew something was wrong. It was the first and only time I have experienced that type of cold feeling from her. She told me that she wasn't ready to be in a relationship like this; she told me that she didn't think she was worldly enough. She told me that she was afraid of getting hurt, but none of it made sense to me, and never did. I was devastated. You know how you can get hit in that little area above your stomach and it knocks the wind out of you?"

She nodded.

"That's how I felt until I had her back."

"What do you think it was?" Kara asked.

"I have no idea. It drove me crazy, because I felt in my heart that she really wanted to be with me, like I wanted to be with her. Maybe her mother thought things were too serious. Maybe I wasn't polished enough. I don't know. It has crossed my mind from time to time."

Kara stared in my eyes for a moment before she spoke up. "I read through some of the letters, and it was nosy, I guess, but sometimes us nosy bodies come up with things." She got up and went to the chest while talking.

"Like I said, I read all of the letters, which was sort of true. There was this one," she said and then turned around swiftly. She was holding a square, cream-colored envelope in front of her, waving it up and down as she talked. "This one I thought I would save for you. I'm not saying that I didn't hold it up to the light to see if I could read some of it, but I didn't think that I should open it."

She took a few precarious steps my way and laid it in my hand.

"I think this one's for you," she said.

I looked at the envelope that she had placed in my hand. The cream-colored stationery was browning around the edges. It was addressed to me at my one-bedroom apartment. There was an eleven-cent stamp in the corner. I was stunned. It was a letter she had written to me over thirty-five years ago, but never mailed.

"Do you want to be alone?" Kara asked.

"Why wouldn't she have mailed the letter?" I asked Kara.

We both looked at each other in a questioning way. I was asking for advice as a woman, not as my daughter. She switched hats quickly.

"Well, it could be for a number of reasons. There is probably an explanation for why she wanted to break up in the letter, but she decided she couldn't go through with it."

We both smiled and looked into each other's eyes.

"You gonna open it?" she queried.

"Yeah, I am, but maybe not right now."

"Why not?" Kara asked. "I think I would have to rip it open."

"Well . . . there may be something in that letter that I want to hear and there may be something that I don't. I think I am going to wait until I am in the frame of mind where I can handle anything." I placed the envelope on the music holder on the piano and stood up.

"Where did you find it?" I asked, looking back and forth between Kara and the letter

"It was under the shoebox in the chest," she said.

"Really. Show me," I said, walking toward the chest.

"It was right here."

She pointed to the bottom of the chest and I looked on in disbelief.

"I've been rummaging in the chest every day this week and there's no way I would have missed a letter laying in the middle of it." I said. "No way."

Kara looked at me shrugging her shoulders as she shook her head. "I don't know . . . after I read the first two letters, I lifted the shoebox out of the chest and the letter was right there. Maybe it was stuck to the bottom of the shoebox?" she asked.

I shook my head and gave her a I-have-no-idea shrug. I certainly didn't want to suggest anything out of the ordinary, even though I was thinking it. The room coming together like it had, the music, and now this letter suddenly appearing were all part of the—and I don't know if I was even comfortable thinking what—something that was happening.

"Are you ready?" I asked.

"Yeah."

Kara walked out of the room and I followed. As I walked up the stairs, I looked down at the room. It was a white box that looked like it had been dropped from out of the sky. This is Heaven's place, I thought.

Chapter 8

Kara and I were at the kitchen table having a great conversation about love and life when the back door swung opened and Kenny stormed in. He slammed the door and stood in the corner of the kitchen with his eyes locked on me as he loosened his tie

"Dad, I need to talk to you."

I knew it was coming, but after Kara last night, the detective this morning, Kara and our whole ordeal in the basement this afternoon, I was tired of intense talk, but I owed him. I knew there were too many unturned stones for him to deal with.

"Okay. You want to talk now?" I asked.

"Yeah."

"I was planning on taking a walk around the neighborhood today, so now seems like as good a time as any," Kara said, getting up.

Kenny didn't acknowledge her remarks. He remained stone-faced.

"If it's alright, I'd like for Kara to stay," I said, looking up at Kenny.

Kenny shrugged his shoulders and Kara sat back down. There was an uncomfortable silence as we all looked at one another. Kenny paced a few steps and then turned to me.

"I feel like you owe me a few explanations. I realize that we're all upset, so if I'm insensitive and out of line, maybe it's me and I'm upset, but I think that you owe me more. You've been acting strangely; I have a right to be concerned. And I also think that you have been pretty short-tempered or even antagonistic with me for no reason, and I don't think that I deserve it. I'd like to know what's going on. There have been a lot of things here lately that don't add up."

I inhaled deeply, trying to fill my lungs with strength and exhale the tension though my nostrils. I nodded and shut my eyes, then opened them again as I began.

"You're right. You're right about everything. First of all, I do owe you both an apology, especially you, Kenny.

That's why I wanted Kara to stay. She and I addressed some of the issues last night and today, but there is more that both of you need to know." I ran my hand through my hair, which had grown to be almost Don King-ish.

"Where do I start?" I questioned them and myself.

"How about with this morning?" Kenny snapped. "Help me with that."

I ran the palm of my hand across my face and smiled briefly, which wasn't well received by Kenny.

"Okay. Kara, this morning at the police station, I got hostile toward the detective and stormed out when he told me that he had a problem with my story. From my positioning at the accident scene, it would have been impossible to see the guys who caused it. I wasn't ready to say what I am about to tell you, for a number of reasons, but the way I handled it was wrong, and I apologize," I said turning to Kenny. I took another deep breath.

"Here goes. After witnessing the collision, I was in a haze as I raced to your mothers' car. When I looked in the window and saw her slumped over the wheel, I started to feel my body shutting down. My lungs, my hearing, my heart didn't seem to be doing anything for me anymore. When I opened the door and her body fell on mine, my heart actually did stop. . . . I was . . . dead for whatever period of time that was. Well, during that time when I was gone, I had an . . . uhhh . . . experience. When I opened the car door, and your mother's body fell on me, it was like one of those horror movies when a skeleton falls out of a closet on to somebody, but it was Marlena, and her body was heavy, too heavy." I buried my face in my hands for a second while I tried to regain my composure. I felt Kara's hand touch my shoulder.

"Dad . . . maybe you're not ready to . . ."

"I am," I interrupted her. "When her body actually fell onto mine, I just collapsed. As I fell down, it was like I was in slow motion, falling slowly to the ground, but I never hit. Then a second or two later when I opened my eyes, I was looking down on the whole accident scene like I was up in a tree or something. I saw Marlena's body, my body, the cars, the whole scene—it was very confusing. I didn't know whether I was dreaming, dead, or what was going on.

"Then I heard two male voices directly below me. I could hear them in the SUV, trying to get it started. To my left, I saw the driver's door open and a lanky black guy, who looked to be in his twenties, get out and try to open the passenger door behind him. Then I saw another guy get out of the front door and they both ran off. Oh, wait! When I told the detective that they dropped something shiny, it was a small bottle that the passenger flung to his right as they started running."

"Did you see his face?" Kenny interrupted.

"No, because I was nearly right on top of them. I could see that he was very dark-skinned." I shut my eyes and covered them with my hand to try to get a better picture of the scene. "He had long hair, almost like an Afro, that was taller on the top, but it was messy. I turned around and saw the ambulances pull up. That scene of those paramedics racing to the side of my and your mother's body was shocking. I mean, it was like going to the movies and watching a film, and you're in it."

"Wait a second, " Kenny interjected. Kara put up her hand and he stopped.

"I'm sorry; go ahead," he said.

"While the paramedics were working on our bodies, it seemed like everything around me changed to blue, and I began to rise like a helium balloon. Everything around me was warm and blue, a silvery turquoise, and Marlena was there, but I couldn't see her. It was the most beautiful thing that I have ever felt. It just takes you . . . up. And then there was the light. A shimmering light, and everything just gets better as you get closer to it. I began to see visions of all of the good times in my life. I got to see each of you being born, me playing with Gramps when I was two. It was . . . I can't describe it. That's the best that I can do. Then I heard her voice, or . . . no, I don't think that I heard her voice, but she was talking to me."

"Mom?" Kara asked.

"Yeah. We were communicating in a way so much richer than words, and so much more clearly. We were able to make each other feel what we wanted each other to know. And . . . and we said goodbye. She told me that it wasn't my time to go, but it was hers, and that she would be there waiting for me when I had done the thing that I have to do here. After that she went on toward the light, and I woke up in an ambulance on my way to the hospital." I realized that I was looking off in the distance as I was talking, instead of at my children. I looked at Kara, who had the same starry-eyed look in her eyes as she did when she was nineteen and in love with Carter or whoever the boy was she had met in school. Kenny was more difficult to read. His face was calm and pleasant, like he wanted to believe me, but wasn't sure.

"I hope you can see why it was difficult for me to share that with the detective. Maybe you can help me figure out a better way to approach the situation," I said, looking at Kenny. He just nodded.

"Okay. I guess this is the next thing or item of concern," I said, looking at my daughter. "Kara, when Kenny told me earlier this week that he was having dreams about 'getting' or 'killing' the guys who ran into Mom—"

"Wait," Kenny interrupted. "To put it into context, I was frustrated that Dad hadn't even returned any of the calls from the detective who has been working on this case. So I asked why he couldn't spend five minutes on finding the guys who caused this family all of this pain, instead of playing the piano all day."

Kara looked down, and then back up at him.

"What? Is there something wrong with me wanting to find the guys who killed our mother? Or is that too insensitive of me?"

Kenny's words seemed to hang in the air before us.

"No, Kenny. It's just that . . . things are hard for everybody right now, and each of us is not going to react the same or the way that we think the other person should," Kara said, placing her hand on his stony shoulder. "It really hasn't been that long."

He nodded. "Alright."

"Kenny, if I said it's wrong, I didn't mean to. The point that I was making was that you were having dreams about solving this crime, which we would all love to see happen. I'm suggesting that you must pursue that because then, and only then, can you free up your heart and mind."

Kenny frowned and looked at Kara. I stopped talking and we both looked at him. He shrugged his shoulders.

"Once again, I'm sorry. Maybe it's the whole lawyer training or wherever I'm at now, but 'freeing your heart and mind' is another example of your saying things that are not like you. The reference to Biblical passages, and this after-life experience, I'm not . . . if you say it happened, I believe you. Two months ago, you would have been dismissing things like that as some staged talk-

Love Notes **149**

show event. That's what's freaking me out, I guess. But dying, seeing your body from above, going up to the light . . . it's consistent with other people who claim to have had life-after-death experiences. I guess that it is your different way of talking and behaving that has me concerned," Kenny finished.

"I am different. I feel different. I see things differently. I feel like I'm seeing things now the way that I am supposed to. Anyway, I'm going to say what I set out to say. I think that when we are quiet, God speaks to us in a way that is right for us. I think that he is speaking to you through your dreams; I think you need to be open and listen. It's somewhere in the story of David—I'll find it for you and give you the chapter. It talks about how God talks to us in our dreams. I think that he is talking to Kara through the visions that she is having, and I think He and Marlena both talk to me through music. I don't have that completely figured out yet. But, if it's okay, I would like to finish our discussion at another time."

"Why?" Kenny said, looking confused.

"Well, that's really it. That's all I know for now."

I stood and turned toward the den to get a drink, but I didn't want to set off a new set of concerns by having a drink in the middle of the day, so I turned back toward the basement. "I'm going downstairs to play a little bit," I said. I got up and dashed out of the room before I could see their reactions.

Once I was inside the piano room, I was relieved. I locked the door and stretched my arms and legs to remove the stress, which had built up from the conversation that I had just had with the kids. The place was a mess. The floor was covered with letters, remnants of the roses, and the note box. I reached for the cummerbund, which was on the floor next to the chest, but I put it back down. I decided that I wanted to leave everything where it was for a while. I wanted to get a feel for what Kara had experienced when she was down here alone.

I paced the room before opening the door and walking out into the main basement area. Under the stairs, I had built a crude wine cellar, which consisted of six wooden crates, stacked on their sides in a pyramid: three on the bottom, two on the second row, and one on the top. As I grabbed a bottle of burgundy I heard what sounded like arguing from the floor above. I could hear the sharp burst of Kenny's voice more than Kara's, even though the sounds coming through the old wooden flooring were muffled. I stood still, looking up at the ceiling as I tried to hear whether they were fighting or having an intense debate. I set the wine on the ledge of the window well and grabbed the paint-speckled ladder, planting it directly below a walnut-sized hole in the floor. I slowly climbed to the ceiling. I grabbed hold of the gritty ceiling beam for support and cocked my head to the side, lifting my ear to the hole.

"I think he's in shock," I heard Kenny say. "He may be suffering from some kind of post-shock disorder. It's not an unreasonable reaction for him to have. I just think that we need to talk to somebody to find out what steps we need to take in case we need to do something," Kenny argued. "Think this whole life-after-death experience needs to be looked into. This is Dad, okay? Meat-and-potatoes Dad. He doesn't talk about after-life experiences and clearing one's mind and soul. There's something wrong here."

"Before you go and try to have him committed . . ."

"I'm not trying to have him committed," Kenny barked.

"It totally sounds like it from over here," Kara said.

"I want what's best for him."

"Okay, let's give him the benefit of the doubt. You didn't read the part of the Bible that he told you to read, so I think you should do that. I think that you ought to go back to the police station and check out the stuff he told you. Was the passenger door on the truck jammed, so the second person had to come through the front?"

"Yeah, okay, but . . ."

"Let me finish," Kara added. "I have seen shows about people who have been legally dead for some time who are revived, and most of them tell a story that sounds just like Dad's. There's this book on it that was out a few years ago called *Going to the Light* or something like that. I don't need to see anything else, because I can feel it. There's something really special and magical going on, and I'm not going to be too bull-headed to experience it."

"Bull-headed!" Kenny raged.

With that, I placed my feet one after another down the stairs of the ladder until I was back on the concrete floor. I didn't want to hear everything they had to say, but I did want to know where each of their heads really were and not just how they acted around me. I grabbed my bottle of wine from the ledge and was walking back toward the piano room, when my eyes locked onto the black La-Z-Boy chair that Marlena made me take out of the den. I set the bottle of wine on the piano and went back out to get the comfy chair. It was tough dragging the heavy recliner across the floor, but I managed. Fifteen minutes later, I was in my room with the door locked, kicked back in the La-Z-Boy with a glass of wine in my hand, looking around the room. It was amazing how the place had come together.

I looked at the letters, the pictures on the wall, and the chest, which was still half full of things that I hadn't even looked at yet. I took a long sip of the burgundy. "You're with me, aren't you?" I asked, looking up at Marlena's picture. I looked at the letter that Kara had found, sitting on the piano. It was calling me. I finished the last of the wine in my glass with one big gulp.

"You want me to read it?" I questioned, looking up at her picture. "Of course you do, that's why you put it in the chest."

I walked over to the piano and picked up the letter. I put it to my nose, as if I was going to smell perfume after all of these years—and I did in my mind. I smelled that light flowery perfume that she used to wear back then.

I carefully opened the letter using a pencil as a letter opener. I put the envelope on the piano and took the letter and my glass of wine over to the La-Z-Boy, and sat down to read the answer to one of my life's greatest mysteries.

Chapter 9

I opened my left eye first and struggled with a couple of stuck lashes before I popped my right eye open. I looked around to figure out where I was. I was in my piano room, in the La-Z-boy, with the taste of fermenting wine in my mouth. The letter was laying on the floor beneath my right hand, which was hanging over the armrest. I must have fallen asleep after reading it for the fiftieth time.

In a million years, I would have never guessed that I could love her any more than I had when she was here, but I did, thanks to Kara finding that letter.

It must have been my imagination, but when I brought the letter to my nose there was an ever-so-faint hint of her perfume. I thought about my letters. It must have been that real rose pressed onto the paper that got her.

I set the letter on the music holder before reading it one more time; words that I was sure I would read a thousand more.

> *Hosea,*
>
> *Make no mistake. You are my one and only love. You are the man that God has made me for. Maybe I love you too much and what I am doing is wrong, but it is what my heart compels me to do.*
>
> *Your dreams are what you are and what you become. Your hints of marriage have made me dream of a home and children, and if we go any farther, I think that could happen sooner than either of us may be ready for. But what does that do for the next jazz piano great? Yes, I think you have greatness beyond what you know.*
>
> *I know that you would put your dreams on hold for me and your family and I can't let that happen until the world knows Hosea Brown. There is too much greatness in you that others have to see. This isn't good-bye forever, but it is good-bye. Don't look for me now; I won't be around. You'll see me when I see*

you on a big stage. I'm sorry. I know that this will be as devastating for you as it is for me, but I don't think that we'll have to suffer too long. I'll see you again, but not now. Like Eve, I feel that God took one of your ribs and made me. He won't let me keep it away from you too long.

In love,
Marlena

Every time that I read the letter I could see her mouth forming the words. I could see her eyes, her smile. I could feel her in every phrase, every word and every letter. I could feel the burning in her heart almost like I did when we were on our way to heaven, and she had to tell me that it wasn't my time.

I got up and shut off the light, then found my way back to the piano bench and sat down.

I sat there in the perfection of total darkness, thinking about her letter, and how hard it must have been to write. How many drafts had she made and trashed before arriving at this one? Had she taken it to the mailbox and turned back? Or did she ask God if she should mail it and he told her no?

She had left me so that I could become great in my musical profession, instead of sacrificing my career to raise a family like I had. I wonder how she felt after I quit the band to work two jobs when she was pregnant with Kenny? I hope she didn't have any regrets, because I didn't have any. I have always felt nothing but blessed by God for allowing me to be with her. I'm glad that we didn't wait until the "right time" and had our wonderful children when we did, even though I knew I was on my way to the top in the music industry.

I thought long and hard about the sentence in the letter where she wrote "she was gone for now," but that I would see her again when I was on a stage playing music—and that wouldn't be very long. She believed in me even more than I believed in myself.

There's something spiritual about total darkness. Maybe it's the oneness with things that you can't see, no matter how near or how far. Even though it was pitch black in the room, I shut my eyes and prayed to God. Then I opened them and looked upward and began to talk to him. "Lord, make my family whole again. Mend our broken hearts and minds. Give us comfort in the eye of this storm. You have the power. You are almighty. I know you have heard my prayer and your work will be done. Amen." I took a deep breath and felt some of the weight being removed from my shoulders.

I fumbled around on the top of the piano before I was able to find Marlena's letter on the music holder. I rubbed it between my index finger and my thumb, feeling its texture like I was feeling a fine fabric. My senses were keener. I could feel the impressions of her writing on the paper as I thought about the words that they formed. What had happened was that we were bonded together forever the first time that we met, and although her efforts to put my musical career first were noble, nothing could keep us apart. As I thought about that, I got a wonderful image of her face, the look that she had before we made love. I was savoring that tender adoring look, when I began to hear the music again.

This time the music didn't start in a distance, but it came boldly from above. I stood and held my arms up in the air, letting it take me from all sides. Entwined in the music was her voice, so soft, like a whisper in my ear. My heart was beating wildly while my very being shuddered. I couldn't control it. My smile turned to giddy laughter as tears streamed down my face. Chills raced up my arms and neck. I hugged the air around me, sometimes rocking as if I had her in my arms. Then like the communication that we had on our way to heaven, she told me to play the music and keep her next to my heart. At first I was stunned, because music like that is beyond anyone's ability, except that Marlena, as always, made me feel that I could play it. I walked to the piano in the midst of total darkness, placed my hands on the keys, and played.

I played the music that she sent me with total perfection, no missed notes and no wrong keys. Hundreds of things rushed through my head, but they were flashes. I allowed nothing to distract me. I heard a thump against the wall outside, but I didn't stop playing. I played and I cried, laughed, and smiled. Some of the tears came from the joy of what was happening, and others were out of love for what I was experiencing; perhaps some of the tears were for people who would never hear what I was hearing. While my fingers pranced across the piano keys, the music came to a halt. I sat there, looking around, but it was over. I took my hands off the piano and let my head drop back. I was exhausted but satisfied, as though I had just made love.

Another thump outside the door interrupted my thoughts. I got up and tiptoed to the door and put my ear to it. There was another sound, which could have been a snort or a sniffle. When I opened the door, I found Kara sitting on the floor. Her back was to the wall and her eyes were red and glassy, as though she had been crying. I kneeled and looked her in the eye.

She smiled and looked deeply into my eyes. "You opened it," she said.

"Yes, I. . . ."

I was speechless. I don't know if I was still in a daze from what had just happened in the room or whether I was stunned that she had surmised that I had opened the letter. Perhaps she had determined that from what she had been able to hear through the door. I got up and went back into the room, got the letter and handed it to her. She took it slowly, without taking her eyes off me. "I knew when I heard the music," she said.

I smiled.

"Did the letter give you the answers you were looking for?" she asked.

I smiled and nodded my head yes.

"Read it," I told her.

I stood over her as she read it word by word. When she was done, she stood up and handed me the letter while shaking her head.

"My mother was phenomenal," she said.

"Yeah, she is," I said.

Kara's eyes showed her reaction to my saying "is," but then her face dropped.

"Yeah, she is phenomenal, was phenomenal, but I didn't really know her like I should have."

"What?"

"Dad, I feel dumb and reading that letter just makes me feel dumber."

"Why?"

She shook her head. "You know why," she said. "I know you know why. All the times that I would talk to her as if she were some simple-minded housewife who lived to cook and clean, and not the phenomenal person who knew what it was all about. She had it, whereas me and my idiot crowd and the people that I look up to don't have a clue."

Kara turned away from me and headed toward the stairs.

"Kara. We are your parents, but it is sometimes hard to view your parents as people who . . ."

"I really wish that I had known her. I could have learned so much," she said, climbing the stairs.

* * *

I stood where I was, looking at the staircase where Kara had ascended, wishing things were different, but they weren't. I went back into the piano room and shut the door. I sat in the La-Z-Boy for a minute and then got back up. I went over to the shoebox full of letters and pulled out the third letter that I had written to Marlena and began reading it.

> *Marlena:*
> *When we first met, you spoke to me with your eyes, and I talked to you with my music, we fell in love before either of us could utter a single word. Our spirits came together and now that we're apart it may take more than words to bring us back together. Your spirit runs through my body, making me yearn for you from within. While you're*

reading this letter know this, at this very moment I am in my apartment telling you I love you over and over again, hoping you can hear me and feel my love.

I hope my saying, I love you sooths your pain and settles your heart. I hope by saying I love you a thousand times, beckons an angel who brings you to me.

Stop reading and shut your eyes. Can you hear what I'm saying, "I"ll love you til the end of time. I hope you never finish this letter . . . I hope you drop it and pick up the phone. If the phone seems too cold whisper my name and I'll hear you in my heart.

I'm yours and you are mine.
Hosea Brown

I was sitting on the bench in a starry-eyed daze when it hit me; the feelings that I had when I wrote the letter were the same as I felt now. The process of love separation is a painful one, which takes time.

I got up and flipped off the light. There was something about the dark-

Love Notes 167

ness that, I found, made my thoughts clearer. I remember thinking that if this letter wasn't the one that would bring her back, it would chip away at her heart and I would have her back with another letter or two. I tried to envision her going to the mailbox and getting my letter. Did she cry when she read it? Just as I was forming a vision of her reading my third letter, I heard the music. Like a beloved relative, it was back. I couldn't tell whether it had just started and I was too preoccupied to notice, but the music was there. It was slower, more sultry, and bolder than before.

I turned on the tiny light over the music holder, found the cassette player, and pushed the record button. I was ready this time. I turned the light off and listened. *"So sweet,"* I mumbled. I put my hands on the piano keys and let it happen.

The music was initially sweet and tender, and then it became bold and sensual, like a woman in a red dress begging to be lusted after. I played it as it came to me, inserting cassette after cassette, to capture it all. Throughout the night, there were knocks at the door; I knew it was the kids, but I couldn't stop. I don't know how well that they could hear, but if they could hear the notes that I was playing they would know that I couldn't stop. I had to go to the bathroom once or twice, but I ignored the urges and kept on playing. I don't know if it was light or dark when the music stopped, but when it did, I remember shutting the key cover, folding my arms across the piano and passing out.

I was in the midst of my dream about ascending to the light when Kenny and Kara awoke me. The light pierced my eyes like tiny needles as I focused on the two of them hovering over me.

"Dad. We've been beating on the door off and on since last night and early this morning. We just wanted to know that you were all right. We heard the piano last night, but nothing this morning, and we thought that maybe something was wrong," Kenny stated with hostility.

"Dad, when we opened the door and saw you laid out across the piano, not responding to our calls and knocks we thought that . . . we thought that something might have happened," Kara added.

There was a long, dead silence. I was curious, but I didn't want to ask them what time of day it was. I had already decided to tell them what was going on with me.

"Your mother was sending me some incredible music and I had to take it down. I mean, tonight it was completely different. I was in the room and . . . ," I stopped talking mid-sentence when I noticed Kenny rolling his eyes and looking at Kara. I thought that after our conversation about what I was going through they understood or at least believed the things that I was telling them, but Kenny's look made me feel like he and perhaps Kara were just humoring me. Maybe they thought I was off my rocker. That hurt.

"Okay. I can see that you guys think that I am crazy." Kara tried to interrupt, but I raised my hand to her and continued. "Maybe I am crazy. Maybe Marlena isn't sending me music. Maybe I am just hearing things, and I am suffering from shock and I need medication . . . maybe. But I thought that you were willing to accept the fact that maybe something special was . . . anyway . . . I guess not. I have to go to the bathroom, so I'm going upstairs. See all of those cassettes?" I pointed to the five or six cassettes on the piano. "I recorded all of those last night from the imaginary music I thought I was hearing. You may want to listen to a few of them. Because if it's gibberish, not beautiful music like I think is on there, send in the guys in the white coats and have them take me away, because I am under the delusion that there is some incredible music on those tapes," I said. I looked Kenny in the eye before leaving the room and heading upstairs.

I felt isolated as I climbed the stairs. I walked past the kitchen, where it looked like someone had cooked something for breakfast. I grabbed a piece of half-eaten toast from a plate and stuffed it into my mouth. When I walked past the mirror on our bedroom dresser, I stopped and took a look at myself. I ran my hand through my hair and then went into the bathroom to get a good look at myself under better lighting.

I flipped on the light in the bathroom and stared at myself in the mirror and thought, "This is what the kids are seeing when they look at me." My hair was four or five inches long on the top and flattened against my head on the sides. It looked like it had become grayer in the last couple of weeks, almost completely salt and pepper. My beard had become rather grizzly as well. I had on a worn-out pair of khakis and a long-sleeved pajama shirt that I had been wearing for the last few days. I took another look at myself in the mirror. This was the first time in the past twenty years that I can recall looking different. I ran a big comb through my hair. With a suit and tie, I thought that I could look either professor-ish or just homeless. I took a pair of scissors and began chopping my hair down to size. The beard would be a two-step process: first a mowing with the electric trimmer and then a close shave with warm cream and a fresh razor.

After shaving off the two weeks of growth and patting my face down with aftershave lotion, my skin felt baby smooth and moist. Almost human, I thought. Trimming the mustache was next. Once the steam from the shower had obscured the mirror, I stopped my facial grooming and climbed into the shower. The beads of warm water rushed over my skin for the first few minutes before the water began to penetrate. I stood still, allowing the water to cleanse my body and soul. I wondered what I might see or hear if the lights were out, so I shut my eyes.

I didn't hear any music, but I did see images of Marlena's face fly by as if they were portraits on thin paper that had been caught up in a whirlwind. I opened my eyes with a smile on my face and began to cleanse my body. Emerging scrubbed and cleaned, as my mother used to say, I lotioned and put on a soft pair of khakis and a crisp cotton shirt. I put dab of oil in my hand and rubbed it in my hair before brushing it back. I clean up pretty nice, I thought, looking into the mirror. I headed out of the bathroom, happy with what I saw.

As I walked into the kitchen, I felt like the accused awaiting the verdict of a jury. Would I be found nutty or not? The house was silent. I peeked out the kitchen curtains and saw both Kenny and Kara's cars, so they must still have been deliberating in the basement. I fumbled around the kitchen and paced the floor a bit, before forcing myself down in a chair and drinking my cup of coffee. The coffee smelled good, like warm vanilla. "The work of Kara," I thought. This is where this family was built. Right here at this kitchen table, meal-by-meal, discussion-by-discussion, joke-by-joke. There I sat with a key family member missing, and two downstairs deciding the fate of another. I wanted those thoughts out of my head. I knew Kenny and Kara wanted the best for me, but something made me feel that they were deciding my fate. If the tapes sounded like a bunch of chatter, what would they be doing right now? Crying? Weighing their options on what should become of their grizzly old man?

I clasped the outside of my coffee mug with both hands to feel its heat soothing my bones. It was eleven o'clock. I hadn't looked at the clock when I came upstairs, but it seemed like they had been down there for a long time. What were they thinking about? Were they saying,

"Dad has become a recluse."

"He practically lives in this cave that he's constructed in the basement here."

"It's not healthy."

"He says that he hears music in his head."

"Not only that, he's saying that he had some kind of out-of-body experience."

"I'm just worried that he doesn't take care of himself. Dad always used to be clean. I've never seen his hair not cut."

I folded my hands on the table and lowered my forehead to them and shut my eyes.

I need to do better for my kids, I thought.

Then I started to see those images of Marlena floating around in my mind again, when one of them stopped and became larger. "Honey, stop your worrying. Things will work out just right," she said, before fading to black.

I opened my eyes and looked around the kitchen and then up at the clock. It was almost noon.

Now I hear voices, I said to myself. *What next?*

I got up and walked over to the basement door, aimed my ear down the stairs, and slowed my breathing so I could hear better.

Nothing.

Not long after I sat back down, I heard the kids' footsteps coming up the stairs. They were slow and steady, like those of a bearer of bad news. My two children walked into the kitchen as if they had just seen a ghost. They walked toward me and stopped less than a foot away.

"Dad," Kenny said, shaking his head.

I looked away from Kenny's face and into Kara's. Kenny, who was never at a loss for words, seemed to be struggling.

"Dad," he said. "I don't know what to say. Kara and I had to pull ourselves away to come up here and talk to you. I bet you have no idea. . . ."

"What?" I said.

"What is on those tapes is by far the most incredible piano . . . no . . . it's the most incredible music that either of us have ever heard," he said, looking at Kara and then at me.

"It's so unbelievable," Kara chimed in. "Dad, at one point I got goose bumps on my arms that were so strong I started shivering."

My eyes welled quickly before small tears crept out of their sides. I stood and hugged them both as hard as I could. I felt like everything was about to be better.

I pulled myself away from them at last. "I've been sitting here thinking that

Love Notes

you two were downstairs making difficult decisions about what to do with your crazy old man."

"No," Kara said, smiling.

I looked at Kenny, who cracked a warm smile.

"See, I shaved and cleaned up so at least I wouldn't look so crazy," I said, laughing.

"You wrote all of those songs last night?" Kenny asked.

"No." I shook my head. "I didn't write those songs. They came to me," I said, giving them an enchanted smile. Kenny looked me in the eye long and hard, as if he were searching my soul for answers.

After some time he broke eye contact and gave me an approving smile. "Can you tell me what that was like?" he said.

Kara pulled her hair back over her ear and gave me her full attention.

I took a deep breath. "Okay. When I opened the letter that you found from Mom," I said, nodding at Kara, "I wanted to be by myself and really reflect on what her words meant to me and what they must have meant coming from her, so I shut off the lights, and that is when I heard the music." I explained to them how it was different last night and how it seemed that Marlena came to me with the music; how she told me to play what I was hearing. Kenny and Kara seemed to be in a trance as they listened.

"So, no," I turned to Kenny. "I can never take credit for writing those songs. They came from God through Marlena, or the other way around."

"Well, she was your inspiration," Kenny inserted.

"If you want to call it that, help yourself," I told him.

"Here's the thing, Dad. Kara and I both think that you really have something here. We both buy lots of jazz and both of us agreed that if we had heard any one of your songs on the radio, we would have run out and bought the CD."

Kara nodded in support of her brother. "Yeah. I can't wait to listen to more. Every song that I heard was not only beautiful, but also touching. I felt that I could feel what was behind the music," she said, giving the floor back to Kenny.

"Kara and I both know people in the business and I think that we should try to get a tape over to them to see what they think," he said.

"Ahh . . . hold on a minute," I said. "You guys are suggesting that I send these tapes to a record company?"

"Well, not those exact tapes, but I am suggesting that we get samples of your music to our friends in the industry, yeah."

I could feel their excitement waning. "I am excited that you guys like the music. I guess I'm apprehensive because . . . well . . . right now I feel like the music is as personal as what Marlena and I might whispering into each other's ears." I took a deep breath and looked at my kids, who looked like they did when they were little and I wouldn't allow them to go to the park.

"Let me have a couple of days to think about it. Okay? I mean, try to understand what is going through my mind."

"Okay," Kenny said. "You think that's just me trying to capitalize on something, huh?" He smiled.

"No." Kara stood. "This is different. You don't hide God's gifts; you share them. Kenny, you'll have to read the letter I found that Mom wrote to Dad to understand, but Dad, why did Mom break up with you after you guys first got together?"

I tightened my lip and looked at her.

"She walked away from the man who she knew God had made her to be with, because she felt that the world needed to experience your music on a level that you hadn't even achieved yet. So now you have music coming out of you that is more incredible than I bet Mom had imagined back then, and you're not sure if you want to share it?"

I was surprised that her tone was approaching anger. She must have notice the stunned look on my face and the surprise on Kenny's.

"I'm not angry," she said, "but I am a bit surprised that there is even something to think about here. I am sure that Kenny will give you all of the time that you need and we will respect whatever decision that you make."

I had nothing to say after that. I looked back and forth from Kenny to Kara, and they seemed to be out of words as well.

"Okay. I am going to go to the bedroom to take a long nap," I said. "I've had a long night."

"That's a good idea," Kara said.

"Before you go, there is one thing," Kenny added. "I told the detective what you said about the passenger in the truck having to get out of the driver's side, and he called me back and told me that the passenger's side door was jammed from the accident, so it confirms what you were saying, but of course it presents some kind of new problem for him."

"What?" I said, feeling the blood race up my neck.

"I didn't mean to get you riled up. What I think his problem is is how you knew about the door."

"Which is really the same problem as before—how I could give a description of the perpetrators from where I was."

"Exactly," Kenny said. "Anyway, I will be downstairs listening to some more Hosea Brown on piano."

"Okay," I said.

"Goodnight," Kara said. Before I could respond, she had her arms around me, giving me a big and needed hug.

"Goodnight."

I walked into my bedroom, dropped my pants, pulled off my shirt, and slid into bed. I tried to think about what Marlena had written to me in her letter, as I had promised Kara, but I was just too sleepy. I mumbled parts of the letter as I wandered in and out of consciousness. *"The world needs to see Hosea . . . "* I caught myself snoring. *"Brown . . . don't look for me . . . you won't find me . . . you'll see me . . . when I see you on . . . a . . . big stage . . . big stage . . . in lights and hundreds of . . . people."*

Chapter 10

I opened my eyes slowly and found the glowing red numbers from my alarm clock staring me in the face. 9:03 P.M. Nine-o-three? I thought. I had gone to bed in the middle of the day; now it was dark.

I felt great. I turned on the light, grabbed a pillow from the other side of the bed, and propped it behind my head so I could sit up and plan my day—or night, I guess. What does it matter if I start my day at nine P.M. or nine A.M.? I quickly accepted the fact that having slept all day meant that I would be up most of the night. I reached into the nightstand and pulled out a notepad and a little dull pencil to begin my to-do list.

1. Decide whether to let kids market the music.
2. Call Johnny G and talk about playing the clubs.

3. Talk to Kenny about the detective's issues.
4. Finish reading the letters.
5. Listen to the tapes and try to replay the music.
6. Sit in the room and listen for more songs.

Looking over the list I knew that I could knock out the first two in bed, right here. I took the easy one first. I pulled my phonebook out of the drawer and found Johnny G's number.

"Hello."

"Johnny?" I didn't know why I asked. I would recognize that dark, raspy voice anywhere.

"Yeah."

"Hosea Brown, brother."

"Hey, man! What's going on?"

"Well . . . a lot," I said

"Yeah. I'm sure. You just don't know what to say when something like that happens. Man. I didn't run up on you at the funeral, because it just didn't seem right; you know how folks do, acting like they tryin' to get credit for being there. I was there, though. You know I was there."

"Oh, yeah ... I know you were there. Thanks. What's going on with you? What are you up to these days?" I questioned, changing the subject.

"Playing my axe. You know. It's been good to me. Got three different bands I play with."

"Yeah?"

"Oh, yeah," Johnny replied. "Why? Don't tell me you thinking about getting back out here, are you?"

"I don't know. I've been thinking about it. I've been playing every day. Sometimes I'll play all night."

"Man, you can't play no mo'. You washed up. Finished. Too old," he said, laughing.

"Man, what are you talking about? I've got a new version of *Swing Thing* that'll give you an irregular heart beat," I said.

"Well, bring it on," he said, through his hearty laughter. "Bring it on."

"Alright, I will, but listen, Johnny; I've been wanting to ask you something.

You still liking it up on that stage? I mean, is it still fun, like we used to have fun?"

"Is who still having fun? Am I still having fun? Listen, I'm a big, gray-haired, rusty old nigra, as they used to say, but I still pull the strings that make young girls sing," Johnny started with his gut-busting laugh and I followed suit. I could see that ear-to-ear smile of his right through the phone. Back when we had the band, Johnny would grin from ear-to-ear from the moment we started our set until we played the last note.

"Alright," I said.

"Now, Hosea. Did I answer your question?"

"Yeah, I think I got my answer. So where are you playing these days?"

"Well, let's see. I play at the Cotton Club on Fridays, the Green Dolphin on Saturdays and Sundays, and I play little odds and ends during the week. If you can check me out at the Dolphin, those cats I play with are younger and I'm the old hand."

"I'll try to make it."

"Well, I'll see you then," Johnny said. After I put down the phone, I could feel the smile on my face. I was thinking about Johnny G and the boys back in the day.

The next thing on my list was figuring out what to do with the music, but it seemed like I must have solved that problem while I was sleeping. The answer was crystal clear. I needed to move ahead with trying to record the music for three reasons: (1) I wanted to do something for Kenny and Kara, and I wanted them to know that it was for them; (2) I felt like the project would bring us together; and (3) Kara was right. Marlena felt in her heart twenty years ago that I had the potential for greatness, and with her sending me the music as she was, it would surely turn out to be as successful as Kenny and Kara had in mind.

I sat up on the side of the bed and thought about my decision and what the possibilities were. I felt good. No, I felt great. This could be the cement to bond us back together again with something fun and inspiring for all of us. Maybe I thought that they just might get a chance to feel what I have been feeling.

It was 9:42 when I climbed out of bed. I checked off the top two items on my list. Everything else that I had to do I could do from the piano room, except talk to Kenny. I looked out of the front window and saw his car. He was still in the piano room, no doubt.

* * *

I approached the piano room. The door was closed, but there was a sliver of light radiating from under the door. I put my ear to the door and I heard the music. My music. I opened the door. There was Kenny, sitting at the piano. The music was playing and he had a letter in his hand when he looked up and saw me. He looked me in the eye and smiled.

"It's beautiful," he said softly, as not to disturb the music playing on the cassette player. "Absolutely beautiful."

"What?" I asked.

"Everything. Your letters, Mom's letter to you, and the music . . . what can I say about the music? Never before have I been able to see music."

"What do you mean?" I asked him.

He froze, shut his eyes, and started moving his head to the music. He opened them and looked at me. "Let me tell you in a minute," he said, putting up one finger.

I looked at my son, who was happier and more relaxed than I had ever seen him. I took a seat on the La-Z-Boy and took another look at Kenny before shutting my eyes and enjoying the music.

I opened my eyes I don't know how much later and saw Kenny reading one of the letters. I shut my eyes again and resumed my listening.

As I listened, it was like I was hearing it for the first time. I had never heard the keys played with such tender conviction. The song I was listening to was based on the fifth letter that I had written to Marlena. I could feel the defeat in the song. The first four letters hadn't worked and I was out of bright ideas for getting her back. The song began with bold low notes that ached with pain. The then song transitioned to a more melodic phase that conveyed my feeling in the latter part of the letter, where I broke down and told her what having had her in my life had done.

The music stopped abruptly, with a mechanical click. My eyes sprung open.

"Dad," Kenny said, spinning around on the bench. "This is from letter five, isn't it?"

My mouth sprung open. I was in utter disbelief.

"I was listening and reading through the letters that were up here, trying to match the feelings from the letter with the feelings that I was getting from the music. It's five, right?" He handed the letter to me. I looked at him and at the letter that he was waving in the air.

"I'm almost speechless," I told him. "I was just reciting some lines from that letter in my head. 'You make my skin warmer. Every day I thank the Lord and everything in the world . . . ' "

Love Notes 191

" 'For playing its part in creating you and bringing you to me' ". He finished my sentence from the letter.

"You've memorized all of these letters?" he asked, his eyes widening.

"No, I don't think that I have, but as I listened to the music that particular sentence popped into my head."

Kenny narrowed his eyes, intensifying the look on his face.

"Dad, after spending time down here reading the letters and listening to this music, I think I understand how personal this music is to you. In a way, I feel like this is personal family business, but on the other hand, I'm challenged by the fact that it's too beautiful and too powerful for us to keep to ourselves. I mean, these songs go right to the heart and make you feel things. And what's so amazing is that without lyrics at all, you get the messages loud and clear. When people hear these songs, it's gonna change them. It's going to change a lot of things."

I listened with enchantment. This was cold Kenny talking. He was one of the people who I think the music had changed.

"I've been down here since you went to bed, listening to the music and thinking. I listened to three songs before I read the first letter. By the third song, I felt like I was crystal clear, what the song was about. That's when I began reading the letters to see if I was right. You know something, Dad . . . at one point I stopped the music and sat here thinking. You don't always need lyrics in music. In a way, I think that it is sometimes a hindrance. And you know what?"

"What?"

"I got it. When I read the letters, I knew that I was right on the money. It sent chills down my spine," Kenny said.

I couldn't stop looking at him in disbelief. Kenny doesn't talk about getting chills and things like that. "Kenny, I must have dreamed the question of what to do, because I woke up with the answer, but listening to you has made me even more certain that I chose the right path. Let's get it on."

"You sure?" he asked, grinning from ear to ear.

"Let's do it. I want to share this music with anyone who wants to listen to it. We have to. I am listening to you and asking, 'that's Kenny?' You've told me that I am talking and acting differently, but listen to yourself," I said to him, smiling.

"Yeah. Well, we're all different after this experience. I've always thought that I was a deep thinker, but I've really been getting into some real deep thinking lately."

"Yeah?"

"Yeah. It's all about the relationships with people in your life whom you care about the most."

"That's it. Or to sum it up, it's all about love. Did you read the letter that your mother wrote?"

"Yeah. Kara told me that if I read anything to read that one."

"Your mother was only twenty-two when she wrote it. Isn't that amazing?" I told him.

"Yeah, it really is." Kenny paused and looked up in the air, then he looked back at me. "What happened to you and your music? Did you just stop playing cold turkey? You've always listened to your albums, and I knew you were really into your jazz, but I never knew that you were such a serious player."

"Well, when you have kids it changes the way you think about everything. I didn't want to gamble your future on the uncertainties of my music career. I had to know that I would be able to provide a stable future for you, so I immediately looked for a career that I felt would provide stability, and the post office was it."

"But didn't you . . ."

"Miss it? There were times, but having you and Kara and being able to provide for you guys was so much more important to me than playing music, that it just wasn't an issue. I have no regrets whatsoever. As a matter of fact, it wasn't until the other day when I was sitting upstairs with you and Kara that I even thought about this piano down here. I had completely forgotten about it."

"Really?"

"Oh, yeah. Having a family changes you like that. If I had a chance to do it all over again, I would do it just the way that I did."

"That's good." He was silent for a moment. "I've never loved anybody like you love Mom. Has spending time down here really helped you deal with losing her? Because in a way I can see it helping, but in another way, I could imagine that it could get lonely down here."

"Help me deal with it? Uhhh . . . yeah . . . it does help me to deal with it, but I do have my up days and down days, like I'm sure you do. It's hard. It's really, really hard. But as far as being lonely, don't worry about that. I'm not lonely in the least bit. You see, once the music came, it came with Marlena's spirit. The music just comes like the rain. I think I know when it's coming, but not exactly. But when it does come, Marlena is with it. I can feel her in the room, it's . . . ahh . . . it's nothing that I could even attempt to explain. You talked about thinking long and hard lately about what's important in life, and I think that's good. I have been thinking long and hard down here myself, and you know what I've discovered?" I took a moment to look deep into his eyes. "I'm not alone. I've never been alone. I never will be alone. I've got my mother, my father, my brother, my aunts, my uncles, my grandparents, and Marlena with me every day, all around me, looking after me wherever I am, no matter what I am doing."

"Wow. I feel like without Mom, I'm lost in a sense. You and Mom are my backbone, and without one piece of your backbone, you are without the support that you need to stand upright."

I had to smile. "Good. Good example. You're right. If you were to lose a piece of your backbone, you would not be able to stand upright, but you haven't, I'm trying to tell you. That piece of your backbone that you think you may have lost is still there, stronger than ever."

We sat and looked at each other, looked around the room, and sat silently for a few moments. I stood up and Kenny followed suit. I gave him a hug and we took a step away from each other and smiled.

"Let's do it." I said. "Let's get our music on."

Chapter 11

The next two weeks were really good. Just as I had hoped, the music was helping us bond and heal together as a family. When we would meet and talk about the project, there was laughter. Kenny and Kara were back to taking the little verbal jabs at each other that brothers and sisters do.

I was replaying some of the songs that I had recorded on the cassettes on the digital recorder, as well as the new ones that came to me. Kenny decided to leave me alone when it came to being in the piano room. One time he even brought me coffee and cookies at two A.M. Kenny told us earlier in the week that his fraternity brother at Max-Flow Records, who he had let listen to a cassette, told him that once he presented the digital recordings to his boss, he was almost positive that we would be looking at a recording contract.

It was about nine-thirty in the morning and I was up, fixing something to eat, when the phone rang. I cheerfully walked to the phone and picked up the receiver.

"Hello?"

"Dad?"

"Yeah. Kenny, hey! How're you doing this morning?"

"I'm fine. I have something to tell you."

"Okay."

"Are you sitting down?"

"No. I am up around the kitchen, making some breakfast. Why?"

"Can you take a seat?"

"Yeah," I said to him as I picked up my mug of coffee and took it over to the table.

"Alright, I'm sitting," I reported.

I heard Kenny take a breath during the long silence.

"Last night they found the guys who did it."

The muscles in my neck tightened until I could feel the blood rushing to my head. My skin became flushed and heat blanketed my body.

"Are you there?" Kenny asked.

Images of the accident scene flashed through my mind: the blinding lights from the truck, the thugs running into the night, me and Marlena's bodies lying on the ground.

"Dad!"

"Yeah, I, uhh . . ."

"They picked the passenger up yesterday afternoon and the driver last night at around eleven."

"How'd they get them?"

"It was from what you told Detective Rayborne. He followed up on what you said about the driver throwing a shiny object away when he was running. They went back to the scene and found a bottle with a shiny label on it. They were able to get some fingerprints off of it and match them to the truck and the guys who did it. They both had long records. The prints on the bottle put them at the scene and the prints on the truck make it an open-and-shut case."

"Wow, that's, uhh . . ."

"They charged the driver with first degree manslaughter and leaving the scene of an accident, and they charged the passenger with being an accessory. The detective doesn't think that the charges will stick with the passenger, but with the driver he says he's got him nailed rock solid."

"Good. How do you feel?" I asked him.

"Well, I feel a lot of things. I'm glad that they got them. I feel like there's somebody who's going to pay for what they've done to us. And another part of me wants to go down to the police station and slip the cop a few bucks to give me five minutes with this guy so I can let *him* see what it feels like to get hit by a truck."

I guess I shouldn't have been alarmed to know that Kenny was still very angry.

"I don't know how I feel. I think there's a big part of me that wants to go down there and put a beating on these guys. When you told me that they were caught, my whole body got stiff and hot. Maybe before, these guys were just these ghostly figures that disappeared into the night, but now they are real people who are in custody somewhere behind bars, and I'm feeling pissed off. These guys demolished a car that obviously had somebody inside and they didn't even bother to look back. They just ran. They just ran like cowards! In fact, when they got out of the truck, there were two bodies laid out on the ground, and these mongrels never even looked back."

Kenny was silent.

"There's a little more to it," he slipped in.

"What?"

"The driver wants to talk to you."

"What?"

* * *

The rest of the day was shot. I went downstairs and tried to play some music, but that didn't work at all. When I shut off the lights to see if I could hear anything, I saw visions of the crash and two young punks running away from an accident where they had killed my wife. I couldn't help but think about trying to get Kenny to not be so angry, and here I was clutching my fist and visualizing my hands around this little punk's neck.

The phone rang a few times, but I didn't bother answering it. For some reason while I was on my way to the den to pour a cocktail, I thought about the old revolver that I had inherited from my uncle Aaron. I poured a swig of brandy into a glass and headed to the bedroom. Just inside the closet on the ledge above the door, I found the key to my lockbox. I opened the box and, underneath a slew of papers, there it was: a snub-nosed .38. I stared at it like I did every time I saw it, wondering if it had ever done more than just scare a few folks. Just as I picked it up, the phone rang. I froze like a kid who'd been caught red-handed. I looked over at the phone as it rang again; I somehow knew that I needed to answer this one. I set the pistol down and darted over to the dresser and picked up the phone.

"Hello."

"Dad?"

It was Kara.

"Hey, honey. How are you?"

"I'm fine. How are you?" she asked. "Kenny told me about the guy who did it wanting to talk to you. What are you thinking?"

"I don't know. I don't know what I think about any of it. I'm angry. I don't know how I'll react when I see him, but I am leaning toward seeing him."

"What? Why? Why do you want to see him? Or better yet, why would you see him?"

"I don't know. Maybe it's a need to face the demon or perhaps a way to get closure? I don't know."

"Well, I don't think that it's a good idea. I think that it could be very upsetting and maybe give you an experience that you don't need right now," she said.

"Yeah. Even though I told Kenny to tell them yes, I still may change my mind."

"Okay. Just remember everybody in your decision."

"What do you mean?"

"Just remember the total picture and the effects of what you do on all of us. I don't want you to get there and get angrier than you had expected and do something."

"We're going to be at the police station. What do you mean?"

"Just give some thought to what I've said. That's all. It's just the three of us now."

Woman's intuition, I thought. My eyes were fixed on the open lockbox and the gun on the closet floor. I didn't take my eyes off them for the rest of our conversation. Kara never explained to me what she was talking about, but I knew. I sat on the edge of the bed and thought about the three of us as a family, before I got up and put the gun back inside the lockbox and turned the key.

* * *

It was 9:57 A.M. when Kenny and I opened the door to the District #1 police station on State Street. Hundreds of butterflies were scurrying around in my stomach. We told the officer at the desk who we were and he motioned to a heavy-set policewoman, who escorted us back to the detective's office.

After a grumbled greeting, Detective Rayborne sat at his desk, leaning back in his swivel chair and espousing his beliefs about law enforcement and this case. He told me about the problems that he had had with things that didn't make sense to him and how he tried to work with them. He talked about how the things I said seemed crazy, and the challenge that he had when they yielded results. I wasn't there to talk to him; I was there to face my wife's killer. I could see the fat cop's lips moving, but I had tuned him out completely.

I snapped out of the blank stare when he started talking about going to see the killer.

"Mr. Brown, like your son has told you, we caught the driver of the SUV and his accomplice. There's no doubt that it's them."

I bit my lower lip and nodded.

"Now, what I want you to know is that this dirt bag has a public defender who thinks he's slick. I've seen this one before. They'll try to get their criminal clients to talk with their victim's families so that they can pretend to show remorse, which they then try to use in court to lighten their sentences. That's what this whole thing is about—using you, the victim, to help them get off a little easier. Is that what you want to do? Because that's what you're doing when you walk in that room. I mean, frankly, I was surprised that you agreed to do it. But I can't say that there's nothing in it for you, because there is. You'll probably wind up with a guilty conscience and a few sleepless nights when you and your kids watch this son-of-a-bitch walk a few years early, thanks to your little chit-chat." He stopped abruptly, breathing heavily through his nostrils as he stared me in the eye. He then reached under the flap of a box of powdered donuts and took a bite of one, showering the table with fluffy white sugar.

I was pissed off at him and breathing heavily as well. I didn't say a thing and neither did Kenny, to my surprise.

"Are you sure that's what you want to do, Mr. Brown?"

I gave a nod and from the corner of my eye noticed Kenny staring at me.

"Alright," the detective said taking a final swig from his dirty mug and setting it down on the cluttered desk. "Let's go visit our little pal." He stood up, reached into his desk drawer, pulled out some keys, and headed for the door.

As I followed him through the long corridors of the station marching step-by-step closer to my wife's killer, I began having intense flashbacks of the accident. The xenon wall of lights that came from nowhere racing toward us like a high-speed train, the explosion of tree limbs and car parts as Marlena's car smashed into the tree, and the scrawny rodent-like figures that slithered out of the truck and disappeared into the night. I snapped out of my trance when the detective came to an abrupt stop in front of a corroded metal door. He turned and looked me in the eye as if to say this is your last chance to back out. I returned the stare. He stuck a key in the lock, pushed the door open and nodded for me to go in first. The room was maybe eight feet by eight feet, with blistering gray paint on the walls. There was nothing but a table, four chairs, and a hanging light.

"I'll be right back with your buddy," he said, shaking his head in disgust.

I fidgeted with my hands on the table, wondering if I was doing the right thing. Kara was against the meeting, the detective was against it, and I could tell that Kenny wasn't for it either.

After fifteen minutes or so, I heard footsteps in the hallway. The doorknob twisted from left to right before the door swung open. "Rat" popped into my head the second I saw him, filthy, smelly rat. He was tall and lanky with skin that was an ashy charcoal color, like he was layered in dirt. He held his head down and away as he walked into the room. It was when he stole a quick glance at me before taking his seat, when I saw the eye. His right eye was glazed over with a bluish, mucousy film and it seemed to be fixed looking up and to the right. The detective sat him down in the chair across from me. He was leaning forward with his scrawny chest jutting out from the handcuffs that stretched his arms behind him. He kept his head down.

"Well, let's hear it," the detective barked.

The rat man brought his head up slowly and looked at me with his left eye, while his right eye was locked onto the ceiling.

"Hey, sir, I'm sorry for what I . . ."

The heat from the anger inside of me began to burn my skin.

I sprung to my feet. "What? You said you're what?" I screamed. "You're sorry? You killed my wife and nearly killed me and you're sorry? I didn't come to hear your apologies, because if you were sorry or felt anything for any human being, you would have walked up to the car to see if you could perhaps have saved somebody from dying, but you didn't. You turned around and ran!" I pounded my fist on the table. The detective took a step back toward the door as if to say that it was all right if I wanted to take a couple of swipes at him. I took a couple of steps back myself, because I was literally getting sick to my stomach from the sight and smell of him.

"Let me tell you one thing," I said. "Heaven and hell are real." I turned to the door. "Let me out of here," I said to the detective.

Detective Rayborne didn't move from in front of the door. "You don't want to go now, it's just getting good."

"Let me out," I said. The detective reluctantly began moving when the scraggly voice came from behind us.

"Everything happens for a reason," he said. My body locked up and my head felt like it was going to explode. I turned around and went for his throat with both of my hands. He threw himself off the chair and onto the floor to avoid me. I stood over him, steaming. Officer Rayborne threw the desk into the wall and out of the way. The rat lay on the floor, doubled over with his hands cuffed behind him. I grabbed a chair and raised it over my head and just when I was about to come down with it, Kara's words from the other day rang in my ears. *Dad, think about how the things that you do will affect all of us.* I paused and put the chair down and looked at my wife's killer who was actually a teenager, laid out on the floor in the fetal position, quivering. I turned away from him and headed toward the door. "Let me out," I said.

The cop didn't move.

"Let me out now," I screamed.

He looked into my eyes and then unlocked the door. I bumped into his meaty torso as I stormed out the door. He stayed inside. "Let me finish up in here and then I'll meet you in my office." He gave me a clever nod that I think was meant to be reassuring. As I walked away, I heard furniture breaking over muffled screams. I accelerated my pace down the hallway to something just under a jog, trying to get myself as far away from that situation as possible.

As I approached the detective's office, Kenny saw me and stood up. I kept marching toward the door. Kenny caught up to me by the time I was at the front of the station. As we walked outside, I told him what had happened. When I got to the car, I leaned over the hood and took a deep breath. Kenny leaned against the hood next to me. He seemed like he may have needed to take a few deep breaths after just hearing about what happened in that back room.

"Why would the guy say something like 'everything happens for a reason' to you?"

"I don't know, but my first reaction was to go for his throat. It made me feel like he was trying to tell me that there was something other than his reckless driving that caused the accident."

"Well, let me ask you this, Dad. Do you think that everything happens for a reason? Because I don't."

I shook my head. That certainly wasn't a question that I felt like answering at the time. "I don't know. I . . . I have a hard time with the concept, because if you believe that everything happens for a reason, it raises a lot of interesting questions."

"I went to see Pastor Watkins last week. I was having a few days where I just couldn't figure out why it happened and why God lets things like this happen, especially to someone like Mom. I don't buy that argument that everything happens for a reason, but Pastor said that everything is in God's hand and that he has his reasons for doing what he does, and we may never fully understand them. But I guess what is so weird about this is why the guy who caused all of this pain and suffering basically told you the same thing that Pastor Watkins told me."

At this point Kenny and I were side-by-side, leaning with our backs against the car, looking into the sky, and trying to make sense of what had happened. I think his mind was finally opening up. I decided that it was time to tell him more.

"There's another piece of this thing that I haven't told you about." Kenny stood straighter and turned my way as I said this. "During that time after the accident when my heart was stopped and I was floating toward the light, your mother was there with me. It was like we got to spend one last moment together to recap everything. It was like a rapid review of our meeting, getting married, having our children . . . just seeing the most special times that we spent together. And the way you experience things when you are over there is very different. Like when Marlena and I talked—and I don't know if we were talking—but whatever it was, how we were communicating it was clearer than ever. I was able to feel what she was feeling when she told me something. Well, I was feeling the joy inside of her with every passing memory, when suddenly I felt pain. It was a dark, awful pain that infected her entire body, and then she told me. She said, 'Honey, I love you with all of my heart and soul and want you right here with me, but you can't keep on. It's not your time to go, it's mine. There are still things that you must do on earth; there is part of your journey that is unfulfilled.' Then I felt a few slivers of happiness come into her when she said, 'I'll always be with you and you with me, but when it's your time to be here with me, we will be together with our love forever.' After that I stopped moving with her toward the light. Then I woke up to paramedics in the ambulance."

I looked over at Kenny and he had shut his eyes for a moment and opened them. "That's really interesting," he said.

"What?" I asked innocently. I wanted to see if Kenny understood why I was telling him this now.

"Well, what's intriguing is the fact that Mom knew that it was her time to go and not yours. How did she know that and when do you think that she came up with this information? I mean, it begs the question once again."

"What?"

Kenny looked at me until I turned and made eye contact with him.

"Does everything happen for a reason?"

Chapter 12

Kenny dropped me off at the house and headed back to work. I felt uneasy and unsettled on the inside. Once I got into the kitchen, I felt like a hole had opened in my heart. I had faced the man who took my wife's life and looked him in the eye. I had played the music that rushed into my head, and things were going fairly well, but beneath it all was a pain that was now bubbling to the surface. No music, no songs, no great conversations, or prayers could fill the void. Marlena was a part of me that nothing could replace. I knew that she was with me, just as I had told Kenny, but I needed her in body.

It had been too long. Like fasting, you can do it for only so long, but when your body breaks down and requires you to have food, no matter what you tell yourself or however strong your mind is, your body has needs and it tells you. My heart, body, and mind were crying for the closeness and love of my wife.

I sat down at the kitchen table and looked around. I looked at the refrigerator and saw her opening the door and looking back at me, offering me something to drink. I looked at the stove and saw her cooking. I looked at the other end of the table and saw her saying grace before dinner. I looked at the doorway and saw her there, smiling at me. Then I looked around and saw nothing.

As I sat staring out of the window, I began to wonder if those psychic readers, like the one I kept seeing on Seventy-ninth Street, could really put you in touch with your loved ones like they say. I reached to the other side of the table, grabbed the local paper, and turned to the want ads. *Psychic Reader Sister Dominique can cure spells, cast away curses, and put you in touch with your lost loved ones. Call now.* "What if it works?" I asked myself. If it doesn't, what have I lost—twenty bucks? I grabbed the phone and dialed the number on the advertisement. After the third ring, someone picked up.

"This is Sister Dominique. I'm so glad you called."

I didn't answer.

"Hello?" Hearing the fortuneteller's voice with her gypsy accent made me feel foolish. I set the phone down in its cradle.

I thought if Marlena could talk to anyone now, I think that she would talk to me, not to some gypsy woman. I got up from the table and walked slowly toward the basement stairs. Maybe she would come to me again through the music.

Once I got into the piano room, I turned on the light and looked around. It was getting crowded in there, I thought. There were flowers, pictures, the chest, the recliner, a big furry rug, Kenny's friend's recording equipment, and a bunch of little trinkets and things. I made my way to the piano and sat down. I took a deep breath, exhaled, and put my head down on the keyboard cover. As I sat there with my head down and my eyes closed, I began willing her to talk to me, comfort me, or something.

"Baby, talk to me. I need to hear you now . . . baby, it's so hard being without you. It's worse than when I had occasionally wondered what I would do without you. I miss you so much . . . I . . . I knew that this was going to be hard, but . . . I don't know if I can do it, baby. I'm supposed to be strong and supportive for the kids, but there's not much of me here to support them with. I need you." After a few minutes I got up and turned off the light.

I sat . . . and sat, while looking around the dark room as if something were going to happen. Maybe I was hoping that she would float into the room like a translucent TV ghost and talk to me.

Even though it was dark, I shut my eyes and prayed. I prayed to the Lord to help me deal with this rough time that I was having, and I prayed for Marlena and the kids.

"Almond cream," I used to call her, because her skin was the color of ice cream of the same name, just a little darker than butter pecan. The first time I took her to the ice cream shop and ordered a scoop of almond cream, I dripped some on her skin and we both laughed because it really was the same color. It was also on that day that I learned she could pack a punch; I grabbed her arm and licked the ice cream off it before she could stop me. I could tell that she liked it; she was just trying to appear that she was keeping me in my place. I loved it. I loved everything that she did. As I reminisced on our times at the ice cream shop, the music came. This time sounds swirled into the room like a breeze through an open window: slow, sensual music that was as bold and as sexy as a woman wearing a silk dress. When Marlena did put on sexy nightclothes, she would always suggest that we go to bed. But once I was in bed, she would take her time, waltzing around the room pretending to do things until I insisted that she get in bed with me. Chills raced across my back and shoulders when I realized that it was the music that was giving me such a clear vision of her. She was talking to me, and I liked what she was saying. I loved it. Then the thought hit me that I wanted to have this experience again. It was as though a light bulb had gone off in my head. I ran my hand along the top of the piano until I felt the cassette recorder. I depressed the second button from the right, which was for recording. I listened for another minute before I began playing what I had heard. Like I said, it was slow and sexy. At one point I thought I heard the words, but I don't think there were words. What I was hearing, I thought, was what she was telling me through the music, but I heard it in my head, like she was singing right into my ear.

> *"The beauty of heaven and the skies are flawed in my eyes without you-o-o, yeah. I'm with you every day in every way. Don't you feel me in the breeze, babee-ee . . .*

There was more, but I feel funny sharing it all. After a few minutes, I pulled my hands off the keyboard and just listened. Playing took away from the experience of listening, and I wanted the whole experience. I got up and moved over to the reclining chair and sat back, looking up toward the heavens. Some beauty can't be described. It was Marlena, now an angel or with angels, sending me the most incredible music, brushed with her love.

I sat in the chair for what seemed like an hour, taking in what had just happened. I thought about Kenny and Kara, and what I needed to tell them. I was ready, and I think they were, too.

After hanging up the phone from working things out with Johnny G, I called Kara and Kenny. I got each of them on my first try, which was amazing. They were both able to have dinner with me Sunday night at the Green Dolphin supper club. I was ready to give them the message that I had received from their mother.

To my surprise, the Dolphin was packed. I figured on a Sunday things would be slow, but Kara informed me that one of her friend's hosted an event there on the third Sunday of each month, called "Stepping on Sundays."

The waitress took us to the elevated table in the corner of the dining room, which gave us a view of the river out back and the band through the glass. The glass around the dining area added to the elegance while reducing the sounds from the band and bar area to a minimum. Kenny and Kara sat across from me. It was amazing to have two children who were so attractive and successful. I began to see myself in Kenny more and more.

Dinner was pleasant. We caught each other up on the week's events. We gave Kara some more details about my visit with the driver, and she filled us in on the reactions that her choir's music coordinator had to one of the songs that she played for him. After our table had been cleared and everyone had coffee or an after-dinner drink, I decided that it was time to say what I had come to say.

"I invited you guys to dinner because I had something specific that I wanted to talk to you about—a few things that both your mother and I feel are very important to both of you."

Kenny's face tightened as he focused, and Kara's eyes widened with interest.

"It's nothing bad," I said, making sure that they didn't get too riled up.

"Good; I thought that you were about to tell us that we were really part wolf or something," Kenny laughed.

Kara gave him a smirk as she rolled her eyes and we all started laughing.

"What?" Kenny asked.

"If Dad told you that you were part wolf, it wouldn't surprise you, would it?" she asked him.

"Alright, alright." Kenny nodded. "So I sowed a few wild oats in my youth, that hardly makes me a dog—but a wolf? No. I wish I had been part of one of those supportive black families, where folks respect one another."

We all had a good laugh.

"Sorry about that, Dad. Go ahead."

"Okay. I may not have the best way to say all that I have to say, but bear with the old man. You guys are the type of children who every parent wishes they had. Think about what you want: a beautiful, intelligent, and classy daughter and a handsome, bright, and dignified son, and who wouldn't love it if these children got along with each other and they loved, respected, and cherished you?"

They both nodded. "That's what I've got, and to me it is what has made my life so rich and fulfilling." I felt a little tear come into my eye, but I quickly blinked it out when Kenny raised his glass and we all tapped it with ours.

"When you have kids, you do everything in your power to make sure that they have a happy life. If you see them going wrong, you jump in and try to steer them right. Now, your mother and I have had some concerns over the years, but it's hard to say whether it's the times that we live in or something that perhaps we've done, but we've been concerned about this: We've felt that you guys are rightly focused on your careers and such, but we have felt that too little was being focused on the real thing that will make you happy in life. And that's love—having a loving spouse and children. Some people say that that's not for everybody, and some may say that that view is old-fashioned, but listen when I tell you. Life without my family is unimaginable. When I was . . . well, I need to just say it . . . even though it feels a bit funny sometimes. When I was on my way to heaven, much of my life passed before my eyes, like watching a big home movie. What's interesting is what I saw and what I didn't. I saw vivid images of my parents, my grandparents, you guys, friends, and Marlena enjoying the best times of my life. What I didn't see was images of the cars that I owned, that Chevelle SS that I hocked everything for when I was nineteen, or my house, cameras, or any of that. It wasn't there, and a lot of people that I knew weren't there. I only saw the people whom I loved, and it made me wonder. What if I only loved myself and some material possessions—what images would I have seen as I went to heaven? I don't know. The path to heaven is paved in the love that you have established in this life; that's the best that I can figure."

Kenny and Kara appeared to be speechless. I was as well. We all took sips of our drinks and pondered what I had said for a few minutes. It was new and profound for the kids, and for myself as well. Even though it was what I had been thinking about, the way it came out of my mouth was so succinct that I felt like I was listening to someone else.

"I have seen how this experience has changed each of you, but let me tell you this: Kara, you could become CEO of your company, I know it, and Kenny, you could rival Warren Beatty for playboy of the century, but those things won't make you happy. Playboys get girls, but they always want more. Why? Because that's not enough. Executives on the fast track always want to take the next step. Why? Because what they have is not enough. People that have love don't go around looking for more, because there's no need."

Kenny cleared his throat, "Dad, Kara and I have had three or four long conversations on this exact same topic over the last couple of weeks, and it's funny how we both took pieces of our experiences with you and the basement thing. We've been taking some critical looks at our lives and our friends lives, and not all of it has been that pretty."

"Well, don't be too hard on yourselves," I told them. "I think that a lot of this extreme focus on career and money is a sign of the times."

"Oh, it has to be," Kara said, "because we didn't learn it from you and Mom."

I reached across the table and grabbed Kara's hand in lieu of a hug. I held it firmly and then reached out and took Kenny's. "I love you guys."

"I love you, Dad," my daughter said.

"Love you, too." That was my son.

"You don't know how wonderful you have made my life. I can see the band getting ready to play, so before it gets too loud in here, there is another thing that I have to tell you, and it is something that I have been holding close to my chest until the right time." I looked deeply into each of their eyes. "These were some of your mother's parting words before she left me and went on to heaven: 'Open your heart and love will find its way inside of you.'"

I tightened my grip on their hands and I felt each of them clutch my hand a bit firmer as I talked. We all had smiles on our faces, as though we had just had a visit from Marlena.

Someone must have opened the doors to the club area, allowing the music to flow into the restaurant. Kenny started bopping his head and singing to the music.

"*Ain't-no-half-steppin'*. Big Daddy Kane," he said, getting out of his seat and dancing. I got up and moved around the table so I was next to him.

"Big Daddy Kane? This was out when Big Daddy Shane was in diapers, boy. You don't know what's happening,"

I said. "I raised you wrong. Ya'll kids don't know nothing about no Heatwave." I started doing my dance that the kids love to make fun of. "This is some seventies groovin' right here."

"I do seventies," Kara said. "I know Heatwave." She stood up and started moving from side-to-side.

Kenny picked up the leather folder that concealed the check and inserted some bills into it before tossing it back on the table.

"I know what time it is, I'm just playing with you. This band is killing it though," Kenny said.

"Yeah. It's jazzy, but real funky," Kara said.

"Yeah. Let's go check them out," I said.

The three of us danced out of the restaurant and into the club area like we were in a Soul Train line singing; *Ain't-No-Half-Steppin.*

I don't think they had any clue what was about to happen.

Chapter 13

The club area was a classic cabaret. There were small round tables covering most of the floor and a well-attended bar on the side. The stage spanned the entire back wall and in the middle was my man Johnny G.

"Hey, you guys remember Johnny?" I asked Kenny and Kara while panning the floor for a table.

Before either of them could answer, Johnny pulled one hand from his guitar and waved. I waved back. He then leaned back on his stool and made a series of motions to one of the waiters and then pointed to us. Whatever he said sent the waiter racing our way.

"You're guests of Mr. Garret?" the waiter asked.

"Yes."

"Come right this way," he said.

We followed him to a round table just to the right of center stage. Johnny threw me a bigger grin as we took our seats.

"This band is really good," Kara said. "He was the one in the band with you when you met Mom."

"He was right next to me, looking almost exactly the way he's looking now."

Johnny sat in the center of the stage with a white electric bass on his knee, surrounded by four other band members, most of who were younger. He was the old man laying the musical foundation, a swing melody on the bass, while the young folks layered it with hip-hop sounds.

"Man, they're good," Kenny added. "Did you know they were going to be here tonight?"

I didn't answer; I just smiled and shrugged my shoulders.

Once they had brought the song to its frenzied close, Johnny took the mike.

"Well, alright now," he said in his thundering voice. "For those of you who don't know, ya' betta ax somebody," he said, breaking into laughter. He reached into his back pocket and pulled out a balled-up handkerchief and wiped the sweat from his brow in between words.

"Y'all feel that?" he said, taunting the crowd. The cheers got louder.

"Yeah, it's something wrong with you if you can't feel that there. I'm Johnny G and as long as I'm up here there will be no half-steppin'. That's what we call new old school," he said. "Old-school jazz with a new-school flavor."

"Done by somebody who's really old-school," a young lady from the band snuck into the mike.

"Can we have some fun in here?" Johnny asked. "Can we have some fun in here tonight?" The crowd roared louder in response. "I want to do something special tonight. I have in the house the guy who taught me how to have fun onstage, and I'm sure that you'll know what I'm talking about when you see him. This is one of my good friends; a true old-schooler who knows how to talk to you right. I'm talking about Hosea Brown. Hosea, come on up here and give us some."

Kara's face lit up and Kenny looked shocked with delight.

"Are you going up?" Kenny asked.

I looked a Kara, who made a little clapping motion with her hands.

I stood and the crowd cheered.

I made my way around the tables and up to the stage. Johnny stood and we hugged for a moment while everyone continued to cheer. I made my way over to the baby grand, while Johnny's piano player gave me an overtly respectful bow before moving to the other side of the stage to the electric keyboards.

Johnny looked over at me and smiled while nodding his head. He leaned into the mike and cleared his voice, which silenced the crowd.

"Brother, it's nice to see you over there at the piano where you belong. I'm yours; the band's yours. Whatcha gonna do?"

I looked at Johnny, the band, and out at the audience, which was now silent. I tapped the microphone. It was on!

"I want to do a song for you that Johnny and I wrote over thirty years ago called *Swing Thing*," I said..

Johnny held up his hand to motion the band to hold back. The song starts with a bass line that seems to ask a question and pauses as if to wait for an answer. When Johnny plays it, he makes the body gestures and facial expressions of someone asking a question. That's what we used to call "Geezin'"; I made that up as a joke with the guys in the band. It's Johnny G playing the bass and cheesing; I just shortened it to *geezin'*. After Johnny's *geezin',* I come in on the piano. The response is fast and commanding. The beginning of the song is about two fellows in a nightclub who see a beautiful woman and talk smack to each other about who has enough rap to get her. All of that playing in the basement must have really honed my skills, because when it was my time, I came on like a storm. The stage was mine and I owned it. I felt like I was twenty-three-years old again, back at the Destiny Lounge, clowning with Johnny and the band. Johnny strolled over to the piano, playing his bass, looking me in the eye as he jammed. It was love.

The second part of the song is a rendition of the guy with the most nerve going over and talking to the woman: This is where the piano does the talking. The crowd cheered me on, and then Johnny pointed a finger at the drummer, who rolled off a slick little solo. The song then took on a smoother vibe, when the real rapping began. Johnny next signaled in the sax player, the other keyboardist, and the flute. He had obviously taught them the song, because it was working. I felt the grin on my own face as we all went to town together. I looked the sax player in the eye like I loved him. I felt like an orphan who had finally found a home. I had completely forgotten about the crowd until I noticed movement out the corner of my eyes. I turned and looked at the crowd, and they were dancing! Dancing! Kara was dancing in place and Kenny was dancing with one of the girls from the table next to him.

We must have played that song for twenty minutes before we finally brought it to a close. I don't know what was going on, but the crowd wouldn't stop cheering.

"Yeah, man," Johnny, said into the mike. "Yeah, man. That's Hosea Brown, y'all." Everyone in the band was now facing me, clapping along with the crowd. I bowed my head appreciatively. I was getting much love, like my kids would say.

Johnny pulled his abused handkerchief from his back pocket and ran it over his face a couple of times. "Since I see y'all liked that, let's see if we can get Hosea to play us something else."

The cheers escalated with a few people in the crowd screaming, "Yes."

"Go, Dad!" I heard Kara scream.

"Hosea. What can I say, brother? It's love, baby. We want some mo'," he said.

I sat there at the baby grand, thinking about what I was going to do. I looked out over the cheering crowd and into the eyes of my two kids.

"Yeah," I said into the mike before I pulled it closer to my mouth. "Thank you. Thank you very much. I haven't

Love Notes   239

been on a stage for quite a while now and I have to say it feels good. Thank you. I have something that I have been playing with over the last couple of weeks and . . . I want to see if you can feel it."

I braced myself in the seat, getting ready to play, when a rush of nervousness came over me. The place was silent and I began to wonder what I was doing on stage. It was a radical change from spending the last couple of weeks as a hermit rarely coming out of the basement to being center of attention on a stage full of young people.

I put my hands on the keys and began to play the song that had come to me the night that I read Marlena's letter, but it was kind of rough. I almost felt like I did when I played the piano in the basement for the first time after so many years. I tried to calm my breathing. I thought about the song and what it was about. As I played and thought about Marlena's words, I felt myself relaxing. "I am so blessed to have the person that God made me for" were the words from the letter that rang in my mind.

I looked out over the crowd and they were silent and motionless. I wasn't sure whether they liked it or not, but I kept on playing. When I got to the part where she was telling me that she was going to leave me, I could hear her voice surrounded by the music that was flowing into my head. I played what I heard, note for note, now that I was into the groove. I felt her warmth around me: She felt different, loving as usual, but nervous.

Unlike the other times when the music had come and stopped abruptly, this time I could feel the song coming to an end like a long farewell. I savored every note as though perhaps it was the last that I would hear this way. When the song came to an end, I was exhausted. Then I heard the cheers from the crowd. I was startled, because I had forgotten all about them. They kept on for what seemed like fifteen minutes. Then they roared again. Johnny G appeared next to me with his white electric bass on his chest, and gave me a hug. The rest of his band lined up on the stage and bowed to me in unison.

I wasn't quite sure what to do. I just sat there, feeling like I should say or do something, but I didn't know what I was supposed to do. Johnny stood there next to me with that big grin on his face, and leaned down next to my face and spoke into the mike.

"Hosea Brown, y'all. Hosea Brown." He looked back at me. "What do you call that?"

I was surprised by him asking me that question. I rummaged around for an answer. I looked out over the crowd and then I looked into Kara's eyes. I grabbed the mike and pulled it back in front of me. "Thank you," I said, trying to be heard over the cheering crowd. "Thank you very, very much." I said. I patted the mike with my hand and it made a thundering sound. I was just checking to see if the mike was working, but the noise that it made silenced the crowd. "Once again I want to thank you for your appreciation of the song. It is a song that is very dear to me, and I can't tell you that I wrote it. It just came to me. Well, let me get up and get out of here, and let you young folks get on with your party."

They clapped again. I stood up and nodded to the band and was turning to the side of the stage when Johnny stopped me.

"You never told us the name of that song," Johnny said.

I turned around and leaned down into his mike.

"I call it *Love Notes.*"

The crowd cheered as I headed off the stage.

Just as I put my foot on the first step, I felt a sharp pain like an arrow piercing my chest. I never felt the stairs or the floor when I crashed down on them.

* * *

Besides what felt like an arrow stuck in my chest, the rest of my body was numb. My breathing became more difficult and I began gasping for air. There was a crowd gathered around me whose faces were all a blur. When I felt that everything in my body was giving up, I heard Kara's voice.

"Oh, my God! Help! Dad! Somebody call an ambulance. Help!"

My eyelids were very heavy, but I strained to open them. Everything was fuzzy, like looking through frosted glass. I could make out Kara and Kenny next to her.

"Dad, can you hear me?" Kenny questioned peering into my face. "We're getting help." I tried to say yes, but it was too hard. I was able to move my hand a bit and I felt Kara take hold of it. I gripped her hand with my last bit of strength and tried to move my lips. She turned so her ear was barely touching my mouth. I gave it all I had. Each word seemed to force that spike in my chest deeper.

"My . . . rib . . ." I paused to build more strength. "I . . . can't . . . live . . . anymore . . . without . . . my rib. I . . ."

I shut my eyes, trying to regain some strength.

"Dad!" Kara cried. I could feel her tugging at my arm, but I didn't have the energy to respond. As I lay there in a daze, I began to hear music. It must have been Johnny and the band. Johnny had probably taught them that the band has to play on to manage the crowd. The music was nice; a whole lot better than their first set. The piano was true and singing to the heart. Whatever my problem was, it was over, but when I got up to get a closer look at Johnny's guy on piano, he wasn't there. Nobody was playing at all. Johnny, all of the band members, and Kenny and Kara were standing on the right side of the stage in a circle. Even though I was above them, I really couldn't see what they were doing. The music was playing, but nobody was at their instruments. Then a crew of paramedics rushed in, parting the crowd, and once they made an opening, I saw my lifeless body.

I was now above the crowd, floating upward, when I stopped ascending. Kenny and Kara were embracing each other while watching the paramedics pumping my chest. Their faces were filled with terror. Kenny pulled Kara toward him and turned her head away when they electrified my body with the paddles, trying to restart my heart. My body jumped from the floor, but then fell back like a rag doll. There were groans from people surrounding the body. Kenny held on to Kara and began walking her away from the scene as he continued to look back with horror. Kenny's head suddenly dropped on Kara's shoulder when the paramedics set the paddles down, signaling their defeat.

"He's gone," he whispered. Her legs buckled. Kenny held her up as he walked her over to the piano and sat her down on the bench.

I took myself over to my kids. I felt their pain, worse than I ever had. I looked back at my body, and it looked stiff and out of life. I wanted to hold my kids, but I couldn't. I tried, but they couldn't feel me.

"Did you hear what he said?" Kenny asked her.

"No!" she screamed out. "No, Dad! No! No, Dad!" She struggled to get loose, but Kenny held her until she collapsed again.

Kenny held his sister with all of his might, as he looked back to witness the paramedics covering their father's body with a sheet. Tears dropped from the corners of his eyes.

Kara stopped her crying for a moment and pulled away from Kenny and looked into his face.

"You want to know what he said?" she asked him. She wiped her tears again before answering. "I can't live any longer without my rib."

Kenny looked confused.

"Remember in Mom's letter when she wrote that she was like Eve who was made from Adam's rib?"

Kenny's jaw dropped.

I looked back at the paramedics, who were now carrying my body away. Kara took her head off Kenny's shoulder and looked around the room and then directly up to where I was, like she could see me. I was right there, hovering over her.

"Goodbye, Dad. I know that you and Mom will always be with us. I love you," she said, wiping away tears and smiling as she looked up at me. I wanted to say something back, to touch her and Kenny one more time, to hold them and comfort them the way they needed.

I put myself around them and tried to hug them or touch them, but nothing happened. They couldn't feel me. I went over to the keyboard and tried to push one of the notes down. I summoned all of the energy that I could muster and all my willpower, trying to push down the key. Maybe that would let them know that I was still with them. I struggled, but nothing. Then I moved over the piano. I concentrated with all of my heart and mind on the key in the center of the keyboard.

When that key went down, their necks both snapped around to look at the piano. They looked at the keyboard with their mouths open as the note continued to ring.

"That was the center 'C'," Kenny said.

In unison they both looked up in the air and smiled as if they could see me. As I smiled back and looked down at their beautiful faces, the music began playing louder. I knew these were the notes that I would hear forever.

Love Notes
Soundtrack

Smooth, sensual, and soulful sounds for the senses by the Chicago Jazz Authority.

THE LOVE NOTES CD

An exciting crossbreed of contemporary jazz and R&B with which combines silky melodies and soulful beats. On this unique hybrid, producer Gerey Johnson assembles a team of the best musicians in jazz today. From the original works like *Love Notes, Silk Dress,* and *Heavens Place* to his contemporary arrangements of classics like Anita Baker's *Angel,* this amazing work of art conveys the essence of scenes and settings from the novel.

This CD is available at finer music stores and online at Amazon.com, Barnes and Noble.com, and our Web site, lovenotesforever.com.

Visit lovenotesforever.com to sample music from the soundtrack and read the lost letters from Hosea.

Discussion Group Questions

1. In the story Hosea tells Kenny that maybe God is talking to him in his dreams, do you know whom in the bible God talks to in his dreams?
2. What was your emotional reaction to the ending?
3. How do you think this experience will change the way Kenny runs his life? Kara?
4. As we learn later in the book about why Marlena left Hosea early in their relationship, was it the right thing for her to do? Would you temporarily leave someone that you loved, so that they could best pursue their dreams or become an asset to society?
5. Of the letters that Hosea wrote to Marlena which one was the most powerful?

6. When Hosea began to hear music where did you initially think that it was coming from?
7. What do you think of Hosea's actions towards the driver of the SUV? How do you think you would have reacted toward him?
8. Marlena kept every letter and note that Hosea wrote to her. Do you keep yours? If so what is the oldest love letter that you have?
9. While on their way to the light, Marlena told Hosea that he had to go back because there were things he had to teach the kids? What were those things? Did they get it?
10. Are Kenny and Kara typical of young adults today?
11. There seems to be a premise in the book that everything happens for a reason, do you agree? If so, what could the reason have been for Marlena to die when she did?
12. Hosea talked about how the brother who came in the club one night taught him how to make his

instrument talk. Do you hear stories in instrumental jazz?
13. Does the music on the Love Notes soundtrack take you back to those special places in the book?
14. What do you think about the ending?